G581: Plague Tales
Book 4 of the Gliese 581g series
Christine D. Shuck

This is a work of fiction. Similarities to real people, places, or events are entirely coincidental.

G581 PLAGUE TALES

First edition. May 31, 2023.

Copyright © 2023 Christine D. Shuck.

Written by Christine D. Shuck.

Also by Christine D. Shuck

Benton Security Services
Hired Gun
Smoke and Steel
Broken Code

Chronicles of Liv Rowan
Fate's Highway

Gliese 581g
G581: The Departure
G581: Mars
G581: Earth
G581 Plague Tales
G581: Zarmina's World

War's End
War's End: The Storm
War's End: A Brave New World
Tales of the Collapse
War's End Omnibus - Books 1-3

Watch for more at christineshuck.com.

Table of Contents

Introduction

G*581: Plague Tales* is a short-story anthology that weaves in and around events set at the end of the 22nd century. You can read this book without having read the first three books, with this simple explanation of plot, although this author gently recommends later reading all of the other novels in the series - if only because I think you will enjoy them and find they "fill the gaps."

The over-arching plot for the Gliese 581 series is as follows...

In late 2099, a group of scientists and explorers leave Earth to discover a new world in the Gliese 581 system. Months after they depart, back on Earth, a bio-engineered pig virus crosses over to humans with devastating results. They are overwhelmed by a deep and endless hunger that does not abate, no matter how much food (or other items) a victim devours. Essentially, they eat themselves to death.

Over 99.6% of the population on Earth, and its colonies on Earth and Mars, perish. Only those with AB negative blood will survive, and they are left with high rates of infertility. And if being left with only 4/10ths of one percent of the world's population wasn't bad enough, there is also the issue of a pesky mile wide asteroid heading their way. One bigger than the asteroid that took out the dinosaurs.

- *G581: The Departure* takes you through the outbreak of the virus, and the aftermath of it, including a saboteur aboard the Calypso far from Earth on its way to the Gliese star system.

- *G581: Mars* invites you to see what remains of the colony on Mars after the ESH outbreak, and the subsequent discovery of the asteroid heading toward Earth.

- *G581: Earth* returns the reader to Earth, where they struggle first with infertility and a fight to rebuild their population, only to learn that with an extinction-level event headed their way, 15 million survivors worldwide is more than 14 million too many.

It is, however, the stories behind the stories that often consumes me, and I hope, you as well. A character walks onto the scene, for a moment, a few seconds, and they are gone. Who were they? What fascinating twists and turns did their lives hold? Their story unknown, untold, until now. Here, in *G581: Plague Tales*, you learn more. Whether it is a familiar scene from *G581: Earth* from a different perspective in *At the Gates*, to a more in-depth imagining of the horror of the ESH virus in *Rock Island Bridge Disaster,* or another perspective of how the moment of impact might affect those left behind in *The Drowning Man.*

Perhaps what captivates you is the world after impact and the struggle for survival in *Casa Oceano,* along with the love and loss we find in the moments at the end of one world and the beginning of another. When loss strips you of your children, your husband, can you find love and hope again? *Ayomide and Ireti* speaks to that hope. There is hope entwined with grief, injustice paired with karma. Twelve stories, from twelve different characters point of view.

Welcome to *G581: Plague Tales.* I hope you will enjoy these short stories as much as I have enjoyed writing them!

- Christine Shuck -

Make Bombs, Not Babies

Spring 2096
Earth - Chicago, Illinois

Psilocannabis was supposed to open your mind and provide an overarching positive, even euphoric, experience for the typical user. For a few, a very few, it had the opposite effect, causing depression and CMS, closed mind syndrome. And then there was Brigid, who seemed determined to blaze a completely unique path, and corresponding reaction, to the drug.

Michael Nix slouched on the sofa, jeans around his knees, too overwhelmed with the post-coital bliss and the accompanying psilocannib high to take the time to pull his pants back on. His lover, however, was on her feet and pacing. No post-orgasm rubber-legged feel for her, oh no. She was angry. Her hands moved in sharp jerks, gesturing out at the world beyond the filthy glass panes of the converted warehouse.

"We have become *irrelevant,*" she spat. "Useless mouthpieces whining about the environment, and asking for a helping of porridge like some stupid child!" She ran out of space in the long, narrow room, pivoted on her heel and paced in the opposite direction.

Nix grinned. She was fucking beautiful when she was angry. Bonus points she didn't have a stitch of clothes on, and her body was lean, muscled, and her tits were perfect, without the tiniest amount of sag to them. *Well, they could be a little bigger. But other than that.*

She halted in front of him, her breath sharp, irregular, her eyes snapping. "What?" She snapped at him. "What are you looking at?"

He grinned wider, licked his upper lip. "A goddess?"

Her expression softened, changed, but just for a moment. "Is sex all you think about?"

His body was telling him to answer yes. In fact, it was already saying it if she would just look a little further south. He forced a serious expression on his face.

"Of course not. The cause, EnviroFirst, we are going to change the world. You, me, and the others."

She looked down then, then back up at his face and rolled her eyes. "Christ, you are so full of shit."

"You are Sekhmet, goddess of war, and I damn well worship you." He insisted, stretching out a little further, sliding his feet out of his jeans and grinning as his smaller head bobbed a hello. "Come back over here. I'll show you how dedicated I am to my goddess and her cause."

A Taste of War

In the pre-dawn hours, Michael woke, reached out and felt for Brigid, but her spot in the bed was empty, the sheets cool to the touch. The psilocannabis was still working its way through his system, but the euphoric effects were fading fast. He found her on the roof, wrapped in a blanket, barefoot. To the east, the glow of the approaching sun spread across the horizon. He wrapped his arms around her, nuzzled her neck. She ignored his advances.

"Can't sleep?"

She shrugged. "Something you said, it got me to thinking."

"Should I get back on my knees for this?" That earned him a small snort.

"Sekhmet, the goddess of war."

"Mm," Nix said, his hands looking for an entrance to the body hidden beneath the blanket, "I definitely should be on my knees."

Brigid pulled away. "I'm serious."

Nix frowned, stopping as she stepped away from him. "So am I."

"They need to know that EnviroFirst is a force to be reckoned with. That things need to change, *now*. Not continue with the same old bureaucratic bullshit song and dance. Actual change."

Nix tried to hide his disappointment. He'd rather enact a change in bed. A new position perhaps, or try out those aerial silks she had hanging from the ceiling.

"Sure, baby. You are a goddess of a leader."

Brigid shot him a look. As usual, he had said the wrong thing.

Sex is definitely off the list for now.

"We need to send them a message."

"Okay. What are you thinking?"

Her eyes narrowed as the sky lit up with the first rays of sunlight. "It needs to be something big, a place known for polluting the environment that has sidestepped all attempts at regulation and cleanup. One known for bribing officials and flouting the law."

"China is big. The communists are greedy." Nix volunteered, thinking of a recent expose he had watched. Several of the massive country's industrial cities had especially egregious track records. Cancer rates had skyrocketed, and the birth rate had declined precipitously in the last two decades, even with the abolishment of the One Child legislation from the 20th century.

Brigid's face lit up, her eyes gleamed with excitement. "Yes!" She turned and strode toward the door, leaving Nix alone on the rooftop to watch the sunrise alone. His stomach signaled it was overdue for tea and some breakfast. He made his way down the metal staircase and found Brigid glued to her tablet, her fingers dancing over the keyboard. She hardly acknowledged the toast and tea, leaving both to cool as she continued to dig deep. It was nearly noon before she came up for air.

"That electronics plant in Shenzhen, the Guangdong region of China. The pollution rates are off the charts and the only way they've stayed open is bribery and corruption." Her eyes had the intense stare that Nix hadn't seen for a while. One that signaled a burgeoning plan and days of obsessive research and planning.

She would come up with some kind of protest that would be effective. The last one had targeted a bottleneck in the only road to a plant on the west coast. Blocked with a few dozen bodies and a handful of cars, it had effectively shut down a plastics plant for weeks. Enough time for EnviroFirst to expose a corrupt politician and threaten the re-election chances of the Republican governor. The ripples from that action had reached as far as the vice-president of the Reformed United States of America, and practically paved the way for the election of a Democratic contender. A relative unknown, Gary Chen, would take office in just two short months thanks to the fallout caused by EnviroFirst's protests.

Brigid is too hard on herself. She is constantly downplaying how strong of an effect EnviroFirst has on hard-hitting environmental issues.

They had met by accident. She was heading a protest, something he found out later, and he was finishing up on the last requirements for his degree in ethnobotany. God, how his father had sneered at that.

"I've spent $200,000 Ameros putting you through college so you could become a goddamn *farmer*? In what world does that make sense?" Isaac Nix had rolled his eyes over the video feed, disgust written all over his face.

Nix had still been smarting over that conversation, just hours before, when he absentmindedly crossed the picket line and stumbled into Brigid Teraby. It had been lust at first sight. Getting laid was usually his response to the past seven years of more or less negative interactions with his dad. Find a woman, get laid, give her lasting memories. He was good in the sack, and he knew it, cultivated it, learned with each new lover. He might disappoint Isaac Nix, entrepreneur, self-made man, multi-billionaire and more - but Michael Nix didn't disappoint the ladies. When he ran into her, literally, they both ended up on the ground. She thought he had done it on purpose, and her face flushed with anger, her finger had jabbed at his chest as he tried to apologize.

There was something about her. A fire in her he couldn't resist.

She wasn't beautiful. At least, not in the stereotypical way. Brigid was rather plain-faced, but she had a fantastic body beneath the plain looks. It was the fire inside of her that attracted Nix more than anything. She wasn't afraid of anything and she would drop everything and fight, with her fists if need be, for what she believed in.

He had never felt more alive than when he was by her side. Whether it was in between the sheets, or manning a bullhorn at a protest, the energy that flowed from her was intoxicating and addictive. He had grown up alone after the accident that took his mother's life when he was just five years old. Alone except for a series of nannies who had come and gone until he was twelve. Soon after that, it was off to boarding school and then college after that. His father had hidden himself away from his own grief by working more hours, longer days, even weekends. Eventually, they had been nothing but strangers existing in the same house. *Thankfully*, thought Nix, *it had been an enormous property*. It had taken little for the two to avoid each other completely for days at a time.

"Bomb."

Nix was pulled out of his daydream.

"Wait,... what?"

Brigid glared at him. "I *knew* you weren't listening to me."

Nix sighed, grabbed the rolling chair from his side of their two-sided desk, and planted himself before her. "I'm sorry. My mind wandered off. Tell me again."

Brigid glared for a moment more before relenting.

"Zane thinks we can infiltrate a Chinese plant and plant several explosive devices. Enough to set off a chain reaction in the coolant tanks and incapacitate the plant, draw attention to the cause, and really put the screws to those capitalistic shits masquerading as communists. We will force them to take us seriously."

Zane was Brigid's half-brother. He was also half-Chinese. His mother had been part of a wave of rich immigrants that had come in after The Collapse and single-handedly propped up the economy of the West coast, and other areas, for decades. Zane was a dick who would choose chaos over calm, and rioting over protests any day of the week.

All Nix got out of it was chain reaction and the first word... bomb.

"But, a *bomb*?"

"Well, technically, a series of them. Small ones." Brigid shrugged.

"Are you fucking kidding me, Brigid?" Nix stared at his lover, whose pale skin flushed with anger at his tone. "You think the way to make a name for EnviroFirst is with a *bomb*?"

"I can't talk to you when you are like this." Brigid snapped. "You sound like your father."

It was a low blow, and one she had to know hurt. "I'm nothing like my father."

"No?" Her mouth twisted. "Let's see, deprecating tone, check. Self-entitled pompous asshole, check. Judgmental prick, check." She smiled, showing her teeth, "Sounds like you didn't fall too far from the family tree, Michael. Just like ole Daddy."

Nix bristled. Brigid had a brutal side to her. He'd seen it, but usually she reserved it for others, not him.

"Fuck you, Brigid."

"Already did that." She pursed her lips and raised her eyebrows. "You were pretty good, for a college boy."

He was out the door, his legs took long strides, powerful, angry, and desperate to put space between the warehouse and him. Damn her. She could be vicious when she wanted and especially put out when anyone, anyone at all, questioned her ideas and plans.

"Damn that Zane." Nix growled as his strides brought him to the edge of the city, blocks away from the warehouse where he normally felt more at home than the house he had grown up in. Zane had done this. He had been pushing Brigid towards increasingly violent confrontations, and now this? The thought of them actually going forward with it was sickening. It was one thing to see a protest get heated, and it was an entirely other thing to bring true violence into the game. How could that possibly achieve any genuine success? They would lose support if they resorted to violence. How could Brigid not see that? Why would she listen to that fool Zane? For the first time, he was seeing a different side of her, and he was sure it had everything to do with poison being whispered in her ear. Brigid was blind to her brother's shortcomings.

Protest in Beijing

The crowd was far bigger than any of them had even hoped for. Chalk it up to four billion screaming Chinese, Nix thought, as he stared at the massive crowd chanting and holding signs. The streets were crowded here, far more crowded than anything he had encountered back home. He glanced over to where Brigid was standing. He had stayed away for two days, nearly three, returning as the sun lowered in the west and the heat of the day was slipping away, rapidly cooling once the sun's rays had deserted the pavement below.

She had said nothing, simply pulled him into her arms and began kissing him, slow and deep. Hours later, sweat beading their bodies, she had told him about the new plans for the protest in Beijing.

"We can remind the people how terribly their business leaders are violating the very environmental programs they took credit for helping to pass," she had said, her finger tracing an intricate design only she could see into his chest.

"And the plant? The... bomb?" Nix asked.

"Shelved." She answered tersely. "We will focus on Beijing first and see how much of a following we can get going. They're stacked on top of each other in the cities, with asthma and other air-quality related illnesses on the rise everywhere. They're desperate for change. And they have the numbers to get it done." She sighed, her fingers ever in motion. "I missed you."

It was the closest Nix would get to an apology. If it could even be considered one.

"What does Zane say to all this?"

He felt her stiffen momentarily, then shrug, before she returned to drawing on his skin. "He wasn't happy, but he'll deal. Better now that I'll put him at the front of the Asian office of EnviroFirst. He *looks* Chinese. Our dad really didn't come through in that mix." She snickered then. "Most think he's full-blooded and that I'm his stepsister. So, why not roll with it?"

That had been six weeks ago. Something more was at play. Something Brigid wasn't telling him. Details he wasn't privy to. Nix suspected Zane was a big part of it, but he couldn't prove it, and it wasn't as if he had ever been one hundred percent inner circle in the organization. Still, it was disconcerting. He'd walked into the room a half-dozen times and talk had ceased, Brigid and the others suddenly busying themselves with tasks, lame jokes, and surreptitious glances. The last of his college classes finished, and he had joined them on the flights out. There were seven of them in four separate planes, all landing in different airports.

"It will arouse less suspicion that way." Brigid had said. "Zane and Leila arrived by ship last week."

The sea of faces surrounding him were predominantly Chinese. He couldn't see Zane anywhere, and Brigid was no longer by his side. Nix held his sign, written both in Chinese and English and chanted with the crowd. It didn't matter that he couldn't speak the language; the intent was the same. He felt the crowd surge around him, pushing his body with theirs. The police force here was a far cry from law enforcement back home. He couldn't see their faces behind the darkened riot gear helmets. Each stood back straight, body stiff, clothed in black under the shining white body armor, batons and more at the ready. He had a sneaking suspicion they wouldn't bother with tear gas. Instead, they would wield their batons and tasers, then follow it up with something more permanent.

Nix felt the crowd move, a body and force of its own, pushing tighter against each other as they crammed into an older, more narrow Beijing street. Among older buildings, shops, restaurants, and more, the streets were now lined on both sides with protesters. Nix found it hard to breathe as the crowd crushed closer and closer together. The police seemed intent on occupying the sidewalk on the south side of the street, where a slick, new office building rose in the middle of the decaying structures. A fat man screamed at the protesters over a bullhorn. Again, Nix cast about for Brigid, for Zane, or any other familiar face. He was alone in a crowd of strangers.

An older man fell, or was pushed, against him. From the bag of food clutched in his gnarled hands, it was clear he wasn't a protestor. Nix marveled at how he had made his way from the hole in the wall restaurant behind him, into the maelstrom of the crowd.

This did not stop the riot police, however. Just as the man looked as if he might edge his way across the street to safety, the sound of guns firing cut through the chants of the protesters. Whether it was rubber bullets or something else, it mattered not in that moment. The reaction was instantaneous. Screams of pain from protesters, a wave of bodies, both those falling to the ground and others scrambling to escape, swept through the crowd. Nix watched as the old man was struck, his body arcing back, the food in his hand thrown into the air. Nix had no time to react as he felt the simultaneous punch of impact into his ribs. The brutal wrench of bodies in the crowd slammed into him and then knocked him and the old man down. He had an instant of clarity. Hard macadam beneath him, grinding into the meat of his jaw, his ribs on fire, someone's foot on his hand. A container had escaped the bag of food, rotating in midair before descending into the crush of bodies, hot soup splattering, small droplets of it burning hot against Nix's face. In front of him, the old man lay on his side, his mouth working, as if he wanted to say something, anything. But the screams, the crack of guns, and all the rest blocked it out. Nix watched as the light in the old man's eyes faded, and whatever made the old man who he was, individual, unique, vanished. It left but a shell behind. He heard the police fire their weapons again, the crowd surging and screaming and falling. A slam of a body into his, hard against his head, and Michael Nix surrendered his consciousness to the night.

You're in the Hospital

Consciousness is highly overrated. No one ever mentions that coming to can hurt so damned much.

When Nix came to, he was in a hospital room. Cultural differences aside, hospital rooms are quite recognizable. So were the zip-ties that secured his left wrist to the bed frame. Nix sucked in a breath and immediately regretted it. The sharp pain emanating from his left ribcage told him he wouldn't be going for a jog soon.

The door slid open then and Brigid's face came into view. "Hey, you're awake." She whispered it, glancing at the door she had just come through. "We have little time before the police come in. But I wanted to check on you."

"I lost you in the crowd." Nix whispered back, his back and ribs screaming in pain as he tried to sit up.

Brigid glanced at the door. "I have to go. They can't find me here. They will haul me in for questioning and Zane's waiting for me outside." She reached over and squeezed Nix's hand. "Look, Nix, when they ask, remember, you know nothing. What happens next has nothing to do with you."

Nix captured her hand in his. No easy feat. It appeared two of his fingers were broken. "Brigid, wait. Where are you going?"

She smiled at him. "Sometimes it takes a violent act for people to wake up to the reality of the violence we do every day to Mother Earth." She cast another glance over to the door, leaned over his bed and kissed him passionately on the lips, and then slipped out of the room before he could raise any more objections.

Shit, shit, shit!

Nix closed his eyes, wincing at the pain that rolled and pulsed through his body. He struggled to pull himself upright. If he could only get his left hand loose from the zip-tie. His right hand on his cheek sufficed only to cause him more pain as his fingers found the raw, chewed up skin where his face had met the pavement. His legs, arms, back and ribs ached and burned. He pulled against the restraints. The zip-ties didn't budge, other than to further cut into his skin.

And then it was too late, far too late, a sharp-tongued nurse was at the side of the bed, her voice loudly calling out, likely for help, because seconds later, two men, obviously part of hospital security, came running in. They helped hold Nix down until his free right hand could be zip-tied in place, and whatever sedative the nurse added to the IV had taken effect.

As Nix slipped into unconsciousness, his last waking thought was of Brigid. She hadn't given up the idea of bombing that plant. Not at all. And he had been a fool to believe she would.

Stupid American

News of the bombing hit less than 48 hours after they transferred Nix from the hospital to a prison infirmary, looked over with a jaded eye and placed in the general population. He could walk, and as long as he didn't move too fast, he could breathe shallow enough that the broken ribs didn't send flashes of agony through him.

The other prisoners left him alone, avoided him, actually. This was no surprise. He was in dutch with the guards and being seen with him likely wouldn't help anyone else. The bombing made it worse. He knew something was up when the whispers and sideways glances increased exponentially. He had been an oddity for a day, then it became business as usual within the metal and cinder block world he found himself in. But now, something had changed. As they had queued up for dinner, with Nix hanging back from the others, he hadn't been particularly surprised when guards descended upon him, handling him roughly as they dragged him away from the mess hall, down a long corridor, steps, and deep into the guts of the prison, far below most prisoners.

Here the lighting blinked to an inconsistent beat. The walls were damp with condensation, and the dimly lit corridor held prisoners in dark, miserable, fetid cages of steel and stone. He could hear one man cough, low, wet. The cough that sinks its claws into you and won't let go. The stench of unwashed bodies and fear permeated the place. Here they shackled him in a dim, damp room. His hands, then his legs, the metal bolted deep into the stone bench that sat before a table with an office chair. Not too close, though. Certainly not within reach, or even spitting distance, were he so inclined. Which Nix most certainly was not. He did not resist. He hadn't. Not since that moment of madness and desperation in the hospital. He sat there, waiting, the cold of the stone and the wet on the walls seeping into him, working at him. They had chained him, then left, the door swinging shut with a groan. Time passed. Hours, possibly. The chains prevented him from laying down, or reclining, or really much of anything other than sitting there waiting on the pleasure of the men in charge.

Nix reviewed his situation with growing dread. He was here on a tourist visa. He'd broken a half-dozen laws by participating in the protest and it was easy enough for the Chinese authorities to tie him to Brigid and the EnviroFirst movement. *Should I have tried to tell them what she was planning? Would it have done any good?*

He waited for so long that his ass had long gone numb, and muscle cramps had worked their way up his back, seizing at intervals along his spine. Despite this, he occasionally drifted off, even if it was for a few seconds or a minute. Just long enough to make reality and consciousness all the worse. He was absolutely and completely screwed.

He jerked involuntarily when the door swung open. Nix wasn't sure if it was day or night. His stomach was empty, his mind blank, and his body wracked with pain from sitting for so long. He watched as two men filed in. One sat, placed his tablet on the surface, and typed. The other stood directly behind the first man, and stared at Nix, his expression stern. The seated man muttered something in Mandarin and the man standing interpreted.

"You are part of the terrorist group, EnviroFirst, responsible for several deadly incidents on Chinese soil over the past two years."

Nix said nothing.

The seated man spoke again, and again the other man interpreted.

"Your lover is Brigid Teraby. She and her brother set off a series of explosions at the Shenzhen plant in the Guangdong Province early this morning. She is currently under arrest and being interrogated for information on other plots by your terrorist organization."

Shit, shit, shit. Nix was totally and completely screwed, and he knew it. There was absolutely nothing he could say that would make any of this better. He kept his mouth shut.

That didn't last what followed next. Time became something he hated, something hard and unforgiving and drawn out. He wished for the oblivion of unconsciousness. Conscious meant a beating was coming. And questions. Questions he couldn't answer because he didn't know what they had planned. So he told them everything he knew. He opened his mouth and let the words pour out. Whether they made sense or even if they applied. In the middle of it, at its worst, he begged. For the beatings to stop. Or maybe even for them to kill him. All the movies he had watched where the hero stays silent, stoic, while enduring horrific torture, that was not him. Nix knew his worth, and they measured it in moments, memories.

He told them about his childhood. His rich father. He promised them money. His dad's prized Bugatti, his watch collection, and pretty much anything else he could think of. He swore, up and down, that he hadn't known of Brigid and Zane's plans, or whether there were any other plans he didn't know of. Amidst blood, snot, and tears, Nix found himself no more important to humanity than the cockroaches that skittered about on the floor. And by the time they relented, brought him to another cell and left him there, with something resembling food but nearly unpalatable, Nix collapsed on the thin mattress and cried himself to sleep. It didn't take long. He was a fool, a stupid American, a patsy, and he had chosen poorly in every way. The voice in his head, the one saying all of it, as he sank into unconsciousness... it sounded exactly like Isaac Nix's voice.

They Need Farmers on Mars

Nix counted at least ten days, possibly more. The beatings had stopped, but they left him there. In the cold, dank bowels of the prison. He could hear snatches of sound when the door to his cell opened or closed, but beyond that, nothing. Until one morning. He only knew it was morning because of the change in food. The gruel from breakfast differed from the watery soup at midday or the noodles served in tasteless sauce in the evening. That morning, shortly after he finished forcing the food down his throat, the guards came. A moment of terror ran through him, especially when they dragged him to the showers, where they had hosed him down and beat him over and over before. He was pretty sure his broken ribs would never heal at this rate.

He winced as one guard shouted at him in Mandarin, saying something like "ko yee foe" over and over and pointing at his clothing. Finally, he realized the guard wanted him to undress. Shaking, he obeyed. "See foodzi," the guard said, pointing at the shower and pantomiming washing himself. Nix did as he was told. They wanted him clean. That was something. *Better than a beating.* He washed in the lukewarm water, lathering up with soap, rinsing, trying to ignore their stares.

Being shaved, however, was terrifying after all he had endured. When the man came at him with a straight-edge razor, Nix reared back in the chair they had pointed to. "Qua hoze!" the man holding the razor repeated and pantomimed running it across his own smooth face. Nix had only a towel around his waist and it had taken all the calm he could muster to allow the man to shave him. On each side of him, guards stood ready with hands on truncheons.

Clean and clean-shaven for the first time in days, the guard handed Nix a clean shirt and pants. Not his, but also not a prison uniform. What was going on? What were they up to?

Down the corridors, past the dozen other cells, up flights of stairs and into the main part of the jail, he was led, hands tied behind him. Nix hadn't thought he would ever be grateful to see the inside of the main level of the prison. Then again, he hadn't ever been in a jail before, and certainly not in the squalid, decaying warren of cells below. Down another corridor, through countless doors, until he lost track of where he was, as if he had ever known to begin with. Finally, a simple room, with a table, two chairs. They removed his shackles and gave him a push toward an empty seat. The door shut behind him, only to re-open seconds later.

Nix blinked at the sight of his father. His presence here made no sense. Isaac Nix was far too busy shuttling from his holdings in Europe and the Americas to come here. And yet, here he was. In the flesh. Nix stared at the man who he shared 50% of his DNA with. Isaac Nix was dressed impeccably, his Bugatti wristwatch peeking out from the edge of his tailored cuffs, held with onyx and diamond cuff links.

"Good morning, Michael."

Nix's mouth worked. Isaac's tone was no different than it had been when greeting him at home, on the rare occasion when Nix would land there for a day or two, before escaping to a friend's or a lover's, anywhere that wasn't home.

"Good morning."

Isaac sighed and set a thick sheaf of papers down on the table. "I need you to sign these papers."

Nix stared at them and looked back up at his father. "What are they?"

"You admit culpability in instigating a riot and plead no contest to having broken half a dozen of their laws, including association with a known terrorist. In exchange, you get to live. But it won't be here, and it won't be on Earth."

Nix frowned, confused.

"A loophole, for unwanted, brilliant fools like you, Michael. You can thank your farming degree."

"Ethnobotany."

Isaac Nix laughed, wryly. "Trust you to argue a point when facing a life sentence at a minimum and possibly a fate far worse." He tapped the papers. "Sign them, please."

Nix reached for the fountain pen. "Where am I going?"

"Mars, Son. You are going to Mars."

Nix wondered if the beatings had replaced his ability to think with a soft-serve sludge. Mars was nothing but domes. Barren, no atmosphere to speak of, populated with dust and rocks. What in the hell could he grow there? As if reading his mind, Isaac had said, "Huygens Outpost is building an enormous Hab dedicated to crops and small farm animals. You can grow your flowers and play farmer, or you can face charges of eco-terrorism, and face a life sentence."

Nix opened his mouth to speak, and his father raised a finger in warning.

"I will remind you, however, that this falls under the Condaga Agreement, and with it, the charges of terrorism of any kind can be a death sentence."

Nix felt a rushing in his ears. Death, for what Brigid and Zane had done. For what he should have known they would do. *I knew something was going on, and I did nothing. Said nothing. I am complicit in this.*

His father leaned in closer. "Michael, take the deal, and you will go into Cryo within 48 hours and ship out on the next flight with the Jupiter Supply Ship. You can use your skills and passions to make a life there for yourself." Nix saw compassion in his father's eyes. Only for an instant, before the billionaire entrepreneur returned to his natural state: cold, dispassionate, and highly effective at saving his only child's life.

Nix signed the papers. He didn't read them. He seized the vintage Aurora Diamante fountain pen his father had carried with him his entire life. A pen that had helped Isaac build empires. He signed his life away, his sight blurring with emotion.

Isaac had stood then. He had reached out and pulled Nix into a tight embrace. His voice was gruff, heavy with emotion. "Be well, my son."

When was the last time his dad had ever so much as touched him? Nix couldn't remember. He had felt his vision blur with tears. He swallowed past his dry throat and croaked, "Thank you, Dad."

Inside the Domes

"Whatcha got, Nix?"

"A guaranteed fun night starting with drinks in the Commons at 1830 with Sheela from Philly." Nix answered, as he typed in the latest measurements on the seedlings here in the Garden Hab. There were over twenty rows of them, each labeled neatly. They filled the other side of the room with lights, racks of seedlings, and bags of compost. Garden Hab had an earthy smell, at odds with the smells in the other Habs.

Denali snorted. "I meant the plants, young buck. What, you run through all the girls here in Hong Kong and gotta branch out now?"

"Hey, she came on to me, man." Nix shrugged, "What can I say? I'm doing my best to improve inter-Hab relations. Besides, the girl has got legs that just don't quit."

The older man snorted again and gave him a friendly shove. "Lemme see those numbers. You are too busy chasing tail."

"Not true. Not at all. The wheat sprouts were thriving in compost mix 5A and 7B, just as I thought they would." Nix countered, grinning at his friend.

Denali frowned; his thick eyebrows bunched up like furry caterpillars.

"Not 6C and 8E? I was sure the nitrogen mix would counteract..."

"It didn't. And they are coming in at nearly 30% slower growth rate, old man. Kind of like your..."

"Eh, eh, careful there, boyo." Denali's tone was sharp, but his smile showed he didn't mind Nix capping on his love life. He was a lifelong bachelor, something the Mars team had known when they first recruited him. Denali was in it for the science.

Nix grinned, ready for more verbal sparring, when his iDent pinged. "Michael Nix - report to Receiving." Nothing was due in. And his reports, typically sent via tablet uplink to Earth, were all digital.

"Jupiter landed last night." Denali said, shoulders shrugging, looking as mystified as Nix. "Maybe that botanist chick back on Earth has the hots for you." A grin crept onto Denali's face.

Neena was edging into her 70s and dedicated to one thing: her work. Nix snorted. "More like she has the hots for you, man. I'll tell her you're a sure thing and I'm sure she'll make an exception for that Martian sand rot you got going on in your crotch."

He left the Garden Hab to Denali guffawing. It was a short walk, and he spent it mulling over who would send anything to him that couldn't be sent digitally. Receiving was a large Hab. It had the largest set of airlocks and most of the traffic was the food stores. Piles of MREs, the much desired junk foods, and cases of alcohol filled the large space. The Jupiter Supply Ship brought deliveries twice a year, four sets of crew members rotating between Ptolemy Lunar Colony and Mars.

Because of the valuable cargo, and the tendency towards some of the older, established Mars settlers to engage in black market dealings, or flat out theft, the area was monitored and restricted to most. His presence in Receiving Hab digitally noted thanks to the iDent chip in his badge.

"Nix! Get your ass over to the office!" The head of Receiving's voice blared over both his communicator and the loudspeakers.

Nix smirked.

Sonia was petite, her hair buzz cut down to her scalp on one side, long braids on the other, with feathers and beads worked into the braids. Assuming she was anything but a badass was a mistake that some made once and never again. She ran Receiving and the airlocks with an iron fist, and made it her personal mission to damage anyone who was foolish enough to abscond with the snacks and liquor. The black market was her fiefdom here in the Hong Kong Hab, and she aimed to keep it that way.

She sat, her feet up on the desk, an envelope in her hands. Despite being in the dustiest part of the Hab, mere yards away from the airlocks, there wasn't a speck of the red Martian dust anywhere in sight. He wasn't sure how she did it, but Sonia's office was immaculate. She gave him a small smile.

He bowed. "Sonia."

"Nix." She ran a delicate finger along the top of the envelope. "I haven't seen you for a while. Getting your kicks elsewhere?"

He smiled at her, slow, sexy. "Jealous?"

"Hardly."

They had gotten hot and heavy a few months after he had landed. She pursued him from the first day he stepped into Receiving and removed the suit. Sonia enjoyed breaking in the new single men, and occasionally the women as well. She ran the darker side of Hong Kong Hab and all under the table deals went through her. Their time together had been fun. He had to give her that. She was a tiger in bed and it had broken him out of his deep, depressive funk. Waking up from Cryo, stuck on an alien planet with no atmosphere to speak of and learning that Brigid had been executed while he slept in Cryo and the Jupiter Supply Ship spun through space toward Mars was hard to take.

He had watched the vid of her execution. Over and over and over. Until it infiltrated his dreams at night and slowed his steps during the day. Sonia had cleared the board, returned him to the here and now. He was grateful for her. She had reminded him that the life he had was no more, but that he wasn't dead either. They had ended as cleanly as they began, when a shipment of new meat arrived.

"You just prefer to be on top." Sonia said, wiggling her carefully shaped eyebrows at him. "I could make an exception, maybe, just once."

The envelope in her hands caught his attention. It looked familiar. The seal, the print type.

"Is that for me?"

"It seems to be." She rotated it in her hands. "Ident, fingerprint open only. Must be important."

He didn't rise to the bait. "Must be." He recognized it for sure. It was from Dad's assistant, Starling Anders. He was pretty sure she had been Isaac Nix's lover, as well. They had kept it discreet, however, and she had always been kind to Nix and absolutely dedicated to his father.

His stomach twisted. *Not a single word from Dad since I got here, and now this?* He couldn't tear his eyes away from the packet in Sonia's hands. What was in it? Could they have reconsidered his sentence? Had his father used his power and money to not just save Nix's life, but to return him to the planet of his birth?

Nix finally pulled his eyes away from it. Met Sonia's eyes, her expression had changed from seductive to curious, measuring. How much of his past must she know? From what he had seen of Sonia, who made a practice of keeping her fingers on the pulse of everything and everyone that moved into and out of Hong Kong Hab, she knew all about his rich father. She knew, and she was considering how to turn it to her advantage. It wasn't the first time he had seen it, and it likely wouldn't be the last, even 56 million miles away from the man, he could still feel his influence.

Sonia smiled then and held out the envelope. They sealed it in secure holoseal tape. Nix took it from her.

"Call me some night, Nix." She said, tilting her head back, stretching in her seat so she showed off her lithe body. "We could have some fun." She winked. "Maybe I'll even let you have a turn on top."

Minutes later, sitting in his Singles Hab, with its narrow bed that doubled as a couch and included an efficiency bathroom and tiny kitchenette, Nix sat down and stared at the envelope. Something that couldn't be sent digitally. Now that was a rarity reserved only for the most serious of occasions. Was this a chance at a trip back? Or something else? After a few moments of stillness, he reached out and placed his right thumb on the reader. Doing so caused a chain reaction, the tape dissolving along the edge of the envelope's flap, which swung open to the contents held inside. The first was a small, handwritten note from William Estes, Isaac Nix's only real friend. A friendship that had lasted a lifetime as they grew up together since nursery school.

Michael-

I'm so sorry you have to hear of your father like this. It was quick, though. A stroke. He was gone before his body hit the floor. His body figured it out a couple of days later.

I know he never told you, but I think you should know. Your father paid one hundred million Ameros in bribes to keep you alive and commute your sentence to a life on Mars. He would have paid every cent of his fortune to save you. Why he couldn't just say that, well, Isaac was who he was.

He was a good man, and a better friend and father than you might know.

Deepest Regards,

-W-

Nix stopped. A headache was moving in, thrumming in the back of his head, and his heart hurt. Dad had never had time or words to spare for him. Yet he had known that his father cared. It just hadn't been within his ability to show it as other fathers did.

And now he was gone. There would be no conversations, no more words, no understanding. No chance to have a father and son moment. Not that there could have been with these millions of miles between them. Not even when they had lived on the same planet, or even in the same house.

Nix opened the second envelope. His name was written on the front in a familiar script.

Dear Michael-

If you are receiving this, well, you know how the saying goes.

Michael, I'm leaving everything to charities. I know you won't care—the money never really mattered to you—and I understand you better in your absence than I ever did when you were here.

When you went after the ethnobotany degree, instead of following me into law or business, I will admit to being disappointed. However, I have come to re-evaluate those feelings. Now, in your absence, so far away from me, I recognize we are who we are, and that you were true to those feelings and deserving of my respect. I read all the reports from the incident; I recognize now that you had done nothing wrong, and nothing worthy of being labeled an eco-terrorist. That fate rests squarely on the young woman you were with, Brigid Teraby. I wish I could bring you back to Earth, but they have apprised me that, should you return, your fate would be that of a prison cell, no matter your innocence. After all, it became an international incident, and the Chinese government is not a forgiving sort. In case you were unaware, they executed Brigid as a terrorist under the codicils put forth in the Condaga Agreement in a Chinese prison the month after you left on the Jupiter Supply Ship.

Forgive me, son, for not understanding you better, for belittling your choice in occupation and giving you the impression that I thought less of you than I should.

Apart from your mother, there is no one I have cared for more. Be well, my son. Find happiness and fulfillment wherever you can.

Your father,

Isaac

Nix swallowed past the lump in his throat. His past was Earth. His future, Mars. There would be no return. And frankly, there was nothing to return to. Before him, a life lived in domes. Somehow, he had to make a life of it. One filled with meaning.

For now, however, he wanted nothing to do with anyone. He turned his communicator over to Do Not Disturb. He sent a terse message to Denali, who served as his supervisor, and told him he was taking the rest of his shift as a sick day. Denali wouldn't bitch. It was the first one Nix had taken since he had arrived at the Huygens Outpost.

He opened the photos on his tablet. Pictures of his mother, gone since he was four. Of his father. Brigid. His friends and life on Earth. He lay in his bunk, a bottle of Mars-brewed vodka in his free hand, and paged through photo after photo.

Tomorrow, he would get on with living his life. Tomorrow, he would leave the past behind. But as for today? Today he would spend with the dead.

Rebecca the Raccoon Saves the White House

OKAY, I'LL ADMIT IT, this might be a strange place to put a children's story. That said, a shout out, with love, to Rocky, a darling raccoon baby we fostered for a month who inspired the addition of a raccoon to G581: Mars *and this story as well, which earns a short reference in* Mars, *the second book of the* Gliese 581 *series.*

When my husband's trip to Lowe's in early 2021 turned into a raccoon rescue mission, I think it was mere seconds before I fell in love. Wrapped in his jacket were two raccoon babies, about the size of five-week-old kittens. I wanted to name them Rocky and Road, because their road to us had already been rough and I have this weird obsession with naming our pets after food or household objects. My family objected to naming the second one Road, so she ended up being named Roe.

We bought kitten formula, these itty-bitty bottles, and did our best. Within two days, we dropped off Roe at the wildlife sanctuary. She was wild as could be and a real screamer. Rocky, however, was quiet, affectionate even, and we ended up keeping her for over a month. I cried when I had to take her to the wildlife sanctuary, even though I knew it was for the best. It had taken her a while to show her wild side, but when she did, we knew we were ill-equipped to give her the best home.

I still miss the feel of her burrowed in my shirt, or her tiny hands gently working their way through my curls. I would write, and she would sleep, content to curl against my warmth. Wherever she is, I hope she is happy.

Dear Rocky, this story is for you.

REBECCA THE RACCOON was a very real raccoon. And yes, she lived in the White House!

The story of how she got to the White House is not mine to tell. However, the following story, while fictitious, *could* have happened. You never really know.

Rebecca the Raccoon loved living in the White House. She was the first official White House raccoon, and she took her duties there seriously. From participating in the Annual Egg Roll, which she found confusing, but fun, to meeting dignitaries, Rebecca enjoyed her life alongside Calvin Coolidge and the First Lady, Grace Coolidge.

She especially loved roaming the halls of the White House in those quiet moments when everyone was sleeping. She loved roaming and could often be found scampering down the streets that surrounded the White House. Truth be told, it drove the guards a little crazy to see Rebecca bolt down the front

path at night. They grumbled to themselves, "A raccoon has no place in the White House."

Rebecca, however, was rather special. Raccoons are smart, but Rebecca? She was smarter even than the average raccoon. So smart that Grace would often talk to her and Rebecca would make special a special "Churr" sound.

"It's as if she knows what I'm saying and is answering me!" Grace often said.

Calvin would nod, half-listening (being the President of the United States is quite a task) and nod, "Yes, dear."

Rebecca also liked to play dress-up. However, she did not like dresses. Not at all. Instead, she would churr and run her hands over Calvin's suits until one day when Grace relented and, with help from her assistant, had an older suit of Calvin's cut down and tailored to fit Rebecca.

Oh, how Rebecca loved that suit!

She especially loved stepping out into the halls and walking on her hind legs. If she did it just right, she would shock and surprise the guards!

The guards were not as pleased. They didn't like surprises. Not at all.

"A raccoon has no place in the White House." Said one of them.

Occasionally, usually in the middle of the night, Rebecca would slip out of her special house set up near the Presidential suite. She would creep down the corridors, empty except for the occasional guard walking through, and she would find her way out of the White House and into the city streets of Washington, D.C. She loved exploring the city and finding fresh places to play and hide.

One day, as Rebecca was returning from a stroll through the city, she heard a commotion coming from the White House. She quickly climbed up a nearby tree and peered over the fence to see what was happening.

To her surprise, she saw a group of sneaky thieves trying to break into the White House! Rebecca knew she had to stop them.

She quickly scurried down the tree and ran as fast as she could to the White House. When she got there, she saw the thieves had already broken through the front door and were making their way inside.

Rebecca didn't hesitate. She bravely ran into the White House, darting between the thieves' legs and knocking over their bags of stolen goods.

The thieves were so surprised by Rebecca's bravery that they dropped everything and ran away. Rebecca had saved the day!

President Coolidge and his wife, Grace, learned about Rebecca's heroic deed and thanked her personally. From then on, they knew Rebecca as the bravest raccoon in all of Washington D.C. and the protector of the White House. And the guard who had thought a raccoon didn't belong in the White House had to admit it then.

"Sometimes, a raccoon *does* have a place in the White House!"

The End.

Rock Island Bridge Disaster

04.15.2099

Kansas City, Missouri

Raj felt his stomach gurgle, rather loudly, to his ears, despite the enormous breakfast he had consumed just an hour earlier. He hoped the group of investors hadn't heard it and instead plastered a large smile on his face, his bright white teeth gleaming as he pointed at the upper deck, a covered lounge where customers could sit and enjoy the view of the river while eating lunch or enjoying a custom blended latte.

The Rock Island Bridge, originally a narrow train bridge, had been converted to a walking bridge some sixty years prior, at the beginning of Kansas City's conversion to a more green, environmentally sensitive city. Now the city was surrounded by a large interconnected set of trails, shopping that could only be accessed on foot, like the bridge, and an extensive light rail system that had helped mitigate the autocar traffic that had threatened the growth and rebirth of the city following the Reformation.

More than half a century has passed since The Collapse, and Kansas City had become a shining star of commerce, green living, and accessibility for all. That was why Raj had invested in the bridge and cultivated the ethnic diversity of the restaurant offerings on the historic structure. He had spent nearly thirty years here, first as one of the restaurant owners, to eventually, during a short economic downturn, purchasing the entire structure and wearing the multiple hats that it took to guide a multi-unit investment to its proper place in the financial heart of the city.

"The view of the river has been improved by conservation efforts over the past twenty years, increasing the stability of the wildlife and water cleanliness standards. Also, the air quality is within A grade range now that two of the more polluting plants were shut down and the pollution mitigated," Raj said, pointing to the remnants of pillars where a chemical plant upstream had once stood. His stomach rumbled again, louder, and he smiled even wider, feeling the edges of his mouth ache with the effort.

The small group, four men and two women, were all dressed in suits. He was trying desperately to maintain his composure, despite the loud rumblings of his stomach. Raj's hunger had been building over the past few weeks, worsening, and his thoughts settled on the growing number of news reports he had read recently. Not the weird virus. It couldn't be that. He was fine.

His thoughts strayed to his parents. *I'm just eating because of the stress, that's all.* His rise in appetite had coincided with his mother's stay in Raheja Hospital in Mumbai. He had visited her and his father there three weeks ago, an emergency trip to India to beg for them to move to the Reformed United States, where he could care for them properly. But Father would have none of it, insisting that he had lived his entire life in India and he wasn't about to leave now.

"You must come home, Raj," he had said, his rheumy eyes locked on his son, "your mother and I need you."

If only Aarav had lived, Raj couldn't help but resent his older brother for his foolish, daredevil ways, dying on some mountain-climbing adventure when he had aging parents and a wife to think about, *then I wouldn't be in this position.* It did no good to think that way, however, and Raj clamped down on the "what ifs" and focused on the job at hand, selling the last three decades of his life and being the dutiful son his parents expected. And if he could get the price he was hoping for, he could turn around the aging high-rise his family had owned for the past half-century and live comfortably for the rest of his life. He tried not to think of the crowds, the press of people on the street. It differed from here, in the Heartland of the Reformed United States. There was room to breathe, to walk down the streets and drive on the roads without the constant bleat of car horns, of fellow human sweat and perfume in your nose. *I've grown unused to life in the city,* Raj thought to himself. *No matter how busy this town has become, it's nothing like Mumbai.*

One investor, a short woman, with flecks of white sprinkling her jet black hair, was staring at him. Had she spoken? If so, he had missed it, lost in thought. Raj shook himself mentally, "I'm so sorry. What did you say?"

"I asked if you know what the disturbance is all about and if it is common," she replied, inclining her head towards the lower deck where the food court was.

Raj realized that there was shouting going on and he walked to the edge of the upper deck, craning for a view of what could be happening. Below, a melee seemed to have broken out. It was an uncommon occurrence, however, and instead of calming as soon as the bridge security officer arrived, it seemed to increase. A woman was screaming now. No, there were multiple screams. Raj's stomach pains were temporarily forgotten. What an inopportune time for a ruckus! He smiled at the investors, fighting panic, "If you will excuse me, I'll just see what this is about. Please, enjoy the appetizers there on the table. My assistant has samples from all of our current food vendors, one of which won a Cibo award last year."

He motioned to his assistant and then hastened away, down the curving steps to the large deck below. A wiry man brushed past him on the way down, sweating profusely, and Raj bit back a comment as the man slammed him into the solid metal rail. It was something he would have to get used to in Mumbai and that was for sure. The man disappeared out of sight, and Raj continued down the stairs, as the commotion below grew in intensity. It did not prepare him for the scene that greeted him.

Raj Chowdhury had been raised in the business world. His father had shown him the ins and outs of proper ownership, teaching him since he was small how to handle the responsibility of managing others, providing the best quality, and how to mitigate loss. Raj had spent his life, first in the high-rise his family had owned and later here, on this renovated and expanded train bridge, creating quality and providing a wealth of services to the people of his adopted community. He had dealt with everything from the odd prostitute or drug dealer to pickpockets, more than a few violent drunks, and the expected malfeasants. But Raj had never seen the chaos that greeted him on the main deck of the Rock Island Bridge food court. It was almost like a riot, except, even in a riot, there are some rules, some direction. He struggled to understand what was happening here. The food court was packed with people, more than he had seen except during festivals and concerts.

Those were busy, challenging even, but usually plenty of fun to deal with. People drank heavier at them, and there were the occasional fistfights, but overall, the atmosphere was crowded yet friendly. Today, however, was something completely different. The people were on edge, desperate even, and the air crackled with fear and tension. There were at least a dozen brawls in progress, something that had completely overwhelmed the four-person security team. Raj stood at the bottom of the wide stairs and took it all in. At Gauti's, which sold the tastiest fish Raj had ever indulged in, three women locked in what appeared to be a fight over the servings of fish, two of them were grappling over the counter, while another three had climbed over, and were scrabbling to get the fish out of the fryers, burning their fingers. The lone male worker was screaming as he clutched his burned face and eyes, a victim of one invader who was at present defending a pile of fish flowing over a paper basket she had clutched in her arms. She was shoving the fish into her mouth, tears streaming down her face, as she choked on the fresh from the fryer fish. She didn't seem to bother to chew it at all.

The next stall over, at the halal meat market, one worker was down on the ground, another clutching his bleeding head, and a group of customers had vaulted the counter and were fighting over the packages of food, one woman repeatedly punching a far larger man, intent on getting at a large container of pickles he had clutched in his hands.

While most of the tables were on the second level, giving customers a wide swath of space to sit and dine in, the lower level had some as well, as well as several cart vendors. Right now, the hot dog and pretzel vendors were being swarmed, a mass of hungry customers surrounding each cart. The pretzel cart was rocking, shimmying back and forth at the press of human bodies that surrounded it and the hot dog purveyor was screaming and cowering as several women reached for the raw and cooked hot dogs alike from the box fridge and grill, consuming them with a voraciousness that both shocked Raj and appealed to him on a visceral level. It was as if he knew it was wrong, this scene in front of him, and yet... he found it appealing in some perverse way that he could not understand.

He wiped the sweat from his brow. The spring air was cool, the temperature couldn't be any higher than 13 degrees Celsius, but he had been feeling overly warm all morning. As he stood there, gaping, more people continued to appear, one on a small motorbike, which plowed into the crowd, felling two men a few feet from the pretzel vendor, the driver simply stepping off of the moving motorbike to climb over the others as if surfing a wave. He didn't count on the wave surging, however, and seconds later disappeared in a trough of human bodies. If he screamed as he was trampled, the scream was lost in the press of bodies and ambient noise, which had risen higher now. A roar of desperation, of hunger, that had no genuine sense or logic, rose from the gathering bodies. They fought, flailed, grabbed, wrestled, and consumed.

Raj felt his stomach twist in pain and yearning. The investors behind him on the second floor forgotten. His concerns over his mother and her cancer treatments fell away. His feet moved of their own accord, pulling him towards the Rana Ghanash sign on the far end of the food courts, his mouth salivating at the thought of their perfect vegetable samosas with a side of chutney sauce. As the screams increased near the pretzel vendor, his feet moved faster, desperate to get to the samosas before the others emptied the two overrun carts of their foods and then set their sights on other prizes.

Like a flock of starlings, the crowd expanded and flowed, a murmuration of hunger without limits. As he passed the pretzel vendor, now on its side, a large metal bucket of cheese sauce burning its way across arms, legs, while simultaneously being shoveled with grasping hands into mouths. Where there had been the professional, motivated to sell the fruits of his thirty-years' worth of hard work, now there was hunger, all-consuming, his mind fixated down to a single point of interest.

Must have food.

Raj picked up his pace, shouldering aside an obstacle. His mind didn't even register the fact that he had knocked a young woman to the ground, or that there were those in the crowd who had noticed his movement, tracking it, and realized his destination was currently without conflict or competition. A large-boned woman pivoted, her hands shoving at the others in her way, aiming in a direct line for the Rana Ghanash storefront, her ham hock legs barely jiggling as she crushed the woman felled by Raj under her own tremendous weight, breaking three of the woman's ribs. She huffed loudly, but maintained a lead on two men, one younger, one older, and both in far better shape. One of them also stomped the young woman, cutting off her scream of pain as two of the broken ribs punctured her lung and blood spurted from her mouth, dulling her outburst into a wet gurgle. She stopped making noise as three more people trampled over her, her body falling limp, no longer moving. A man stopped long enough to pluck a small piece of pretzel clutched in her hand and swallow it whole before he changed course and began climbing over the large group of people currently fighting for access to the ice cream shop's coolers.

As Raj arrived at Rana Ghanash, his feet slapping the pavement in a full run now, he vaulted the counter, shoved the new employee out of the way, and began devouring the samosas in the tray to his left. The girl fell, stunned, and then scuttled out of the way; her eyes as wide as saucers at the rush of the people that followed him. It was her first, and last, day on the job. Mere seconds later, the large-boned woman had caught up, the counter shaking as she attempted to vault it, failed, and screamed wordlessly as others did with their bodies what she had failed to do.

Raj lasted three glorious belly-filling minutes before a dark-skinned black man snarled at him, slammed Raj's head against the grill repeatedly and ripped the last of the samosas from his hands. Behind him, a skinny white teenager was digging through the trash, consuming food, wrappers, anything his hands landed on.

As Raj lost consciousness, a pool of blood forming around him, his last thoughts were not of his mother and father back home in India. They weren't of the investors waiting on the second level. They weren't even of his mistress, a beautiful blue-eyed raven-haired temptress that his parents would never accept. All he could think of, as he lay there on the ground, trampled, bloody, and dying, was of the maddening hunger. What he wouldn't give for another samosa.

Grocery Run

03.12.2099
Overland Park, Kansas

"Honey, I can't find any fruit for Lily in the kitchen." Charley's mom, Andie stood in the doorway of the tiny closet turned office and peered at Lily. When her husband Bill had left her in her sixth month of pregnancy, Charley hadn't had many options. Ending up back at home had been a stopgap measure that had turned permanent when Dad passed away just weeks before Lily had been born. Mom had been catatonic with grief. That had all changed, however, after Lily's birth. Mom had come alive when she held her granddaughter for the first time. And her world had been firmly centered on her ever since.

Andie was slight, her gray curls swept up in a small ponytail. Charley's hair wasn't much different, except she still had all of her color. It was a mousy brown with red highlights that showed up only in sunlight. She had freckles, a nod to Dad's genetics. He'd been blessed with red hair and freckles.

Charley sighed, "I know, Mom, I just got a notification from Am-Mart that there is some shortage of fruit and the shipment is delayed."

Andie tilted her head, sighed, and said, "Honey, I know you don't want to go to the HyVee after what you saw, but Lily just loves her fruit and she's at that stage where nothing else will do. I don't know what to give her. She just keeps pointing at the fruit bowl and crying for a 'nana.'"

Andie handled caring for Lily during the day while Charley worked at her customer service job, a telecommuting job she had held for the past four years. It paid the bills, and she didn't have to commute, both winners in her book. She could spend her breaks and lunch with Lily, and Andie handled the naps and meals. It wasn't what Charley had envisioned when she became pregnant, but not that bad of a life.

It wasn't as if she hadn't known how he felt. Bill had told her from the beginning that he didn't want kids. Never mind the fact that he wasn't about to put his pleasure aside a single iota, "That's kind of your thing, Charley," he had said once. "I mean, all you gotta do is take a pill. Worse case, you go get it taken care of, right?"

And she had agreed. Until she messed up taking the pills when a nasty flu hit.

A few weeks later, when the nausea of pregnancy took over from where the flu had left off, she hadn't believed it. And a few weeks after that, hearing a heartbeat, well, it had changed everything for *her*, but not so much for Bill. Plenty of arguments later, he filed for divorce. She'd been too heartbroken to ask for his help, and after Lily was born, far too protective. If he didn't want her, fine. Lily had her, and she had Grandma Andie, and that was enough. They were enough. No man need apply.

She hadn't even tried to date. Mom needed her, and so did Lily, and her days were full of both.

Mom wasn't leaving.

"Perhaps I should go to the store," Andie said, chewing on her lip, a sure sign of anxiety. She rarely left the house, except to go to the park down the street. Every day, when the weather was above 50 and below 100, she would take Lily to the park along with Dipsy, the terrier they had adopted last year from the local pound. Andie had recovered from losing her husband enough to care for Lily, a job she excelled at, but visits to the store or other places would see Andie shaking and fearful before and after a trip. Charley had learned to live with it, and not try to change her once brave and adventurous mother. It was what it was, and they all adapted.

Charley sighed again. She removed her earbud and signed off of the program on her tablet. "It's dead, anyway. It's been a ghost town for the past two weeks. I'm surprised they haven't reduced my hours. I'll go now."

"Are you sure, Honey?" Andie nibbled on her lip again. "I know what you saw was awful and you..."

"Mom, I'll be fine," Charley cut her off before Andie set the pot of memories on full boil. "It was just weird and disturbing and, and I'll be fine."

Lily appeared then, fully costumed in a three-year-old's version of Mouse Princess from Mars, her latest obsession. The glass fishbowl on her head crumpled the mouse ears and her voice was distorted inside of the glass, "Mama, I da Mouse Princess, see?"

Charley grinned at her daughter. "I see that, Pumpkin."

"I not Pumpkin, Mama, I da Mouse Princess!"

"Yes, of course you are." Charley planted a kiss on the outside of the glass. "And you are a very brave Mouse Princess. I will get you plenty of fresh fruit from the store, brave Mouse Princess, so that you can eat apples with your peanut butter and jelly for lunch."

Lily frowned, her lower lip transforming her pretty little face into a pout. "I want cookies, Mama."

Charley's stomach did a flip. She hadn't been able to even *look* at cookies since the incident. Just the thought of them made her nauseous. She forced her lips up at the corners, "We'll see, my brave Mouse Princess. We'll see."

Thank goodness the cookies were in the *middle* of the store. She would avoid it like the plague. Anything, *anything* to stop from remembering that poor man on the ground. Charley hugged her daughter, stood up, and reached for her purse.

"Maybe you should go to the corner market instead," Andie said, a hand on her granddaughter's shoulder as they followed Charley to the front door. "They might have apples."

Charley shook her head. "New owners, Mom. The freshest thing they have there are Twinkies." She smiled at her, "Don't worry, I'll get in and out of HyVee in a flash. No worries!" She slipped out of the front door and closed it firmly behind her. The autocar was there at the corner, its engine running, and she pressed her iDent card against the door reader and heard the door lock disengage. She climbed inside and the door shut gently behind her. "HyVee on College Avenue, please."

Zido, the standard autocar interface, responded, "North or south?"

"South location, please."

"Please engage the restraint system," Zido intoned, "Arrival at the destination in thirteen minutes."

"Thank you, Zido." Charley clicked her seatbelt in place and then grinned, remembering riding with Bill. He would tease her constantly, reminding her it was a machine and did not require "please" or "thank you." She had always said, "Even machines appreciate politeness."

It had been nearly two weeks since Charley had ventured out of the house. She had purposely avoided watching the news ever since that first night. After giving her statement to the police, she had taken Lily back home in shock. She had barely spoken to her mom, much less the neighbor, and turned off the vidscreen the minute she walked in the door, cutting short the broadcast. Charley didn't need a vapid reporter repeating with barely disguised glee what she had just witnessed. She could never forget the sight of it, after all.

Lily hadn't really understood *what* was happening, thank goodness. Charley had pulled the cart away, backing up quickly, running over toes and pushing through the crowd behind her just as the blood spread from the man's mouth. Before that moment, it had rooted her to the spot, horrified, fascinated, and unable to fully comprehend what she was seeing.

And after, it had all seemed too horrible to want to remember, although it seemed her destiny was to remember it all too well.

Mary, her neighbor, had tried to ask for details the next day, when it was all over the news. Another person eating themselves to death. Eating and eating until there was no more room, no way to shove another single ounce of food down into their already bulging stomachs. It made no sense, really. Charley remembered reading about how the human body has mechanisms in place to stop us from continuing to eat.

It was why the Romans would vomit, then begin again. It was the only way to keep pushing food down into your stomach.

Charley stared out of the window of the autocar as it moved silently down the street, stopping momentarily at the intersection, before turning left and zipping to the far-right lane. It fell behind a line of other autocars, each equidistant to the other, silently gliding down the road, moving with an efficiency that human drivers could not maintain, towards its requested destination. Her eyes fell on a man in a suit, bent over a trash can and ripping through it, shoving what looked like rotten food into his mouth. Her stomach flipped again. He didn't *look* homeless. His suit was clean, his hair neatly combed, and his shoes appeared brand-new. So, what was he doing over the trash can? Charley closed her eyes and shook her head.

I didn't see him eating garbage. He was probably just throwing the last of his breakfast away. Still chewing, not eating garbage. Surely not.

A few days ago, she had gone online and learned that the man in the store had been a paramedic. The police had quickly identified him as Mac Dolan, and he had had contact with Edith Hainey, an employee of EcoNu who had gone crazy a few weeks before and caused quite the scene at a fast-food restaurant when she drove up, naked. She demanded and then consumed several combo meals in the drive-thru before dying there in her car. The media had certainly changed their tone - instead of painting Edith Hainey as a nutcase; they were now speculating whether she contracted some new weird virus. One that then passed to the paramedic and anyone else who had contact with her.

It had been enough for her to order all the family's groceries online through Am-Mart. And then shortages began. That and the shutdown of the online order system "due to staffing shortages."

I'll just go in and get what I need and get out. Easy peasy. It will all be fine.

Charley closed her eyes and tried not to think about Mac Dolan, or Edith Hainey, or that weird guy in a suit who was eating garbage. Surely, she hadn't seen that. Who would do that, anyway?

All she wanted to do was stay at home, but Lila *needed* fresh fruit and she knew Mom wouldn't say no to a bottle or two of Chardonnay. She grinned a little, her eyes still closed. Lately, after Lila was in bed, the two of them would sit down in the tiny living room and enjoy a glass or two and play a few rounds of pinochle, Dad's favorite, before he passed.

The autocar turned from the road. There was a minor bump, and from the change in speed, she could tell they had arrived. A pleasant tone issued from the autocar's speakers and Zido spoke. "You have arrived at your destination, HyVee, on College Avenue. Will you require return services?"

Charley opened her eyes. "Yes, please. I shouldn't be over twenty minutes."

The door slid open. "After shopping, please proceed to the autocar parking zone three-zero-five," Zido intoned, and the door slid shut behind her.

There were more than the usual number of shoppers for a Tuesday morning. In fact, it felt more like it would on the weekend. The parking lot was *full* of autocars, a line of them occupying the waiting zone, while another line formed behind her, waiting to drop off their occupants. As she walked into the store, she found that the shopping carts were down to the last three in the very back of the cart pickup area. Charley blinked in surprise.

Was it a holiday?

As she walked down the aisles, her surprise turned to fear and her steps became quicker. There was no milk, no eggs or flour, and when she reached the produce section at the far end of the store, empty shelves greeted her. The store shelves were shockingly empty. Just seeing the empty bins was disconcerting. Her stomach rumbled in response, as if the mere suggestion of less was enough to make her hungry.

Power of suggestion. Jeez!

Around her, she could see plenty of shoppers with empty carts milling about. Some looked confused, others stressed out. A man walked by, no cart, clutching a reusable shopping bag in one hand, his other hand to his mouth. As he did, he bumped into Charley. He didn't apologize, just shot past, speeding past the others, heading for the far end of the store. She had been that way first. He would not have any luck there.

Charley turned instead toward the inner aisles. The pre-made foods, the fruit gummies and roll-ups would have to do. Lily wouldn't complain, she loved those foods. Probably more than she loved fresh fruit, for all that Andie insisted she didn't. Charley smiled to herself. Her mom was great at self-deception. When Charley was growing up, the house was well-stocked with a plethora of fresh fruits and vegetables, but her dad had kept a secret stash of junk food and shared generously with Charley behind Andie's back.

Kids love sweet, salty, and fat-filled foods. It's got to be instinctual.

She arrived at the snack aisle and her smile fell away.

You have got to be kidding me.

There was nothing. Not a thing left on the shelves, except... her steps quickened, eager to reach the lone box of Kidz Froot Snax she saw pushed to the back of the bottom shelf. She reached in, pulled at the box, and frowned. It was empty. Her stomach grumbled in discontent.

Charley straightened, glanced around at the stunningly empty shelves, and headed for the next aisle. Canned fruit would work in a pinch. Even canned vegetables if need be.

A woman snatched the empty box from Charley's hand. She frowned and shook the box at Charley. "I'm telling security you stole these."

Charley stared at her. "What?"

"You stole them. You ate them all, didn't you?" The woman advanced toward her, shaking the box at her threateningly. "I'm *hungry,* damn it."

Charley backed away. It was only now, close up, that she could see the woman's nails bitten to the quick. Abandoning her cart, Charley backed down the aisle, slamming into another person as she did so. The man was on the floor, scrabbling at the bottom tier of the shelving, desperate to reach a half-deflated bag of chips at the back, wedged and caught between the metal shelf and wall.

"Watch where you're going, bitch!" He snarled, grabbing the bag, swiping at the chips that flew out of it. Charley stumbled away, her eyes flicking from the woman in front of her to the man at her feet. A half-scream of longing, hunger, or god knows what issued from the woman's throat and Charley jumped out of the way as the woman threw herself towards the man, clawing at the chips.

"Give me those! I'm *hungry*. Can't you see how hungry I am?" The woman's fingers curved into angry, grasping claws. One raked the man's cheek, the other scrabbled at a broken sliver of a chip.

Charley's heart was pounding so hard she could hear anything past the blood rushing in her ears. She turned then, running for the exit, as other shoppers, looking as desperate, if not more so, than the two grappling over the stale remnants of chips on the floor, piled into the aisle, attracted by the noise, and hunger, of their own.

Charley ran on. Past the end cap where two children were attacking their mother, biting her as she screamed and fought them over what looked like a bag of coffee, the grounds spreading in every direction. She ran past a group of people fighting over a bag of food in the parking lot, the owner of the bag, bleeding and unconscious on the ground.

Forget bananas. Forget any of this shit.

She ran to the autocar lot, shaking, her heart pumping, out of breath, found the correct autocar and slid into the seat. A half-second after stuttering the command, "Zido, please take me home," a body slammed against the glass of the door. The man looked half-crazed and his fingers scrabbled at the door latch. Charley had never been so thankful for auto-locks.

"Let me in. You got food, didn't you? Let me in. Let me have some. I'm so *hungry*. Let me in. Let me in, you awful..." The rest of his words lost as the autocar moved away.

Charley sobbed in fear, hunched in the middle, as far from either side of the car, and the windows or doors as she could get. Zido's chime reminding her it recommended a seatbelt continued to sound.

The autocar moved into traffic seamlessly. And the store and parking lot quickly faded into the background, lost from view. Charley rocked herself, tears coursing down her cheeks.

What in the hell is going on? What is wrong with everyone?

Slowly, the tears stopped, her rocking slowed, and Charley calmed. Whatever madness was happening, it was over. She got away from those lunatics. She might not have found bananas or, well, anything, at the store. But that was okay. There was plenty to eat at home. Lily would just have to deal with it. No little girl had ever died from want of a banana. A pony, perhaps, if the old poet Shel Silverstein was to be believed, but not bananas. Charley forced herself to sit back, to stop rocking, and to relax. She was almost home. Lily, and certainly her mother Andie, didn't need to see her so upset over some silly kerfuffle at the grocery store.

God, people can be so weird over food.

Her stomach growled. God, she was so *hungry.*

Nothing Like This

10.12.2099
New York City, New York

Mercy Hospital was the lone remaining hospital in a city filled with the dead. Beth couldn't understand *why* it was still open. The ESH virus had turned a once-vibrant city into a graveyard. Months after the initial outbreaks, they were still finding bodies, still burning them in Central Park. Outside, the air was fetid, even now with fall upon this part of the world. The mornings were chilly with a tang of burned flesh, and the nights smelled like barbecues from hell.

I'm not sure why *they think it's better to burn the bodies at night. You would think it would be less of a spectacle during the day.*

Not that people watched. They had all had their fill of death, after all.

Our cups runneth over in the death department.

If there was any consolation for Beth, it was that, now that the ESH virus had burned itself out, she could return to what she did best, catching babies. An important job. Even more so than before.

Mom has certainly shut up about me somehow "contributing to the overpopulation of our planet" as a NICU nurse. Now it's somehow God's work. Savior of humanity, nursing the innocents to life nonsense. Good lord.

Beth tried to ignore the wave of exhaustion that crashed over her. It was just past two in the morning, and she was halfway through her second shift. The ESH virus had devastated the staff at Mercy, leaving Beth and a handful of others struggling to keep the floors covered. Before the virus, it was an unusual day for her supervisor to assign her anywhere but the NICU. Now, however, she was one of a handful manning the entire maternity ward.

She didn't mind as much as she thought she might. It was a refreshing change of pace to be in the labor rooms with the expectant mothers. Beth appreciated seeing the whole breadth of it, from labor to delivery to postpartum. At least she *had* looked forward to it. Now? Not so much.

Something was happening, however. Something that no one seemed to want to talk about or acknowledge. In the vast city, Mercy Hospital was the only one still standing, still functioning with any real capacity for healing. And even with all the death, all the loss they had all seen, the nursery should be full of babies. They filled every other floor to the brim with the sick and injured. And here in the maternity ward, there were plenty of women in varying stages of pregnancy. The nursery and the NICU were barely populated, and women's cries and screams filled labor and delivery, though not in joy or anticipation. They cried, wailed, keened in sorrow as the tiny beings in their wombs ceased to move, to kick. Their heartbeats stopped.

In the past month, the numbers of fetal deaths and late term miscarriages continued to rise exponentially. Some women experienced it at a few weeks or the first trimester, others in, again, unprecedented numbers during the second and third trimesters. Even the women who had children from successful earlier births were experiencing skyrocketing rates of miscarriage and stillbirth. And in the few cases of live births, at least 20% of the live births died within a week of being born.

Right now, there were three women, all at term, laboring to deliver their babies. Babies they would never see draw their first breaths, or hold close as the baby slept in their arms. Their milk would come in, though. Which seemed like such a cruelty with no child to place at their full and aching breasts.

Beth moved between the rooms, checking on them, touching each woman gently, murmuring reassurances. They all knew, or at the very least their bodies knew, what needed to happen. But birth has its own timeline to completion. All she could do was keep checking in, and then be there for each woman when her time came.

"Christ, this is depressing as hell." Ander muttered as the wails from room 7 continued. Tara Hughes had lost her three children, her husband, in-laws, and her father and half-siblings to the virus. She had given birth five hours ago, and the boy had lived long enough to take two shallow breaths before expiring. "Can we give her another sedative?"

"Not until Dr. Marley gives the okay, and he's with Melissa Turner right now." Beth answered.

"The one who has… I mean, *had* twins?" Ander shook his head. "We need another doctor on the floor."

Beth shrugged. "There's no one else to cover. The other departments are all short-staffed. Even with them closing the oncology department due to staff shortages. I hear all the oncology patients are being told to head to Sloan Kettering in Jersey for treatment or go without."

Ander groaned. "It just gets worse and worse."

Beth sighed. "Tell me about it. I've been working double shifts, four of them a week, for three months now. I just sleep here instead of trying to make it back home. I've forgotten what my apartment looks like."

Ander patted her on the shoulder. "With the hurricane that blew through here last month, you probably no longer have an apartment. Weren't you in a basement unit?"

"No, that was Evie. I've got a second-floor unit. Last I heard from my roommate, there's been a population explosion of rats and it smells like rodents and death 24/7."

Ander snorted, "Christ." He paused, stared off into the distance, and opened his mouth.

"Don't say it, Ander."

"Don't say what?"

"Don't parrot the party line. It isn't the last vestiges of the virus. This isn't ending. And it *isn't* dying off." Beth said, bitterness rising.

Ander glanced at her, quick, and looked away. He'd warned her plenty of times. It wasn't his thing. He cared for her. He was her friend, but as far as the rest of it, it had just been something they both needed. That's how he had put it. A momentary "fuck you" to death. They had only slept together the one night. A frantic coupling in the midst of the pandemic, nothing more. It had resulted in a plus line on a stick a month later. In between bouts of helplessly trying to care for ESH victims and women and their babies dying in droves in the maternity ward, Beth had found her first trimester a nonstop rollercoaster of nausea.

Just when they had gotten to a lull in the virus, a mere week of calm before another round of infections began, Ander had sat Beth down and told her he would be there for her, for the baby, financially at least.

"It isn't what you deserve, and I'm sorry for that. I'm not looking to settle down, Beth, but I promise you I'll be a father to our son, and help care for him." He'd said it so earnestly, a warm hand covering hers. Three days later, cramping and spotting, she'd had him run the Doppler over her four month pregnant belly. The heartbeat, once so strong, was silent. And Beth, who had only let herself become excited after the first trimester came and went, had dissolved into tears.

I should have moved departments. It's been so hard seeing others lose their babies.

She felt every loss, like it was her own all over again. And the losses kept mounting. Still, she stayed.

"Your own experiences are coloring this." Ander said, bringing her back to present. Three months and she still missed what could have been.

"Stop swallowing the lies and look at the numbers, Ander." Beth hissed as Ander looked around nervously to see if anyone was within hearing distance. "This isn't normal, this isn't average. No matter how you cut it, the virus did something, *changed* something, and as if 10.5 billion people dying in less than a year wasn't bad enough, this could actually be worse." She leaned closer. "What if it has changed us on a genetic level?"

"Jesus, Beth, listen to yourself." Ander placed his hand on her arm. "It's a virus. It can't rewrite DNA."

"In the early 2020s, they believed that roughly eight percent of the human genome was comprised of retroviruses. It turned out to be closer to eleven percent. Earlier, before that in the 1990s, scientists discovered a protein called syncytin, which is produced by placental tissue. It plays a role in defining the boundary between the placental and maternal tissues, creating a critical barrier between mother and fetus which both allows for the exchange of nutrients and protects from disease and rejection."

Ander rubbed his eyes tiredly, looked away from her. "Okay."

"When researchers looked closely at the sequence of syncytin, they discovered it was strikingly similar to a known viral protein called env. That protein allows a virus to fuse with a host cell and exchange material."

Ander interrupted, "Yes, I read that paper. It basically suggested that a fetus is like a virus in how it interacts with the maternal host."

"Right. Endogenous retroviruses have infiltrated our DNA over generations and co-opted the functions for our benefit."

"But there is no benefit to sterility, fetal death, or stillbirth." Ander countered.

"Nor is there any need for an appendix, hence a small part of our population developing appendicitis."

Ander rubbed his eyes harder. His eyes weren't the only sign of his exhaustion, the gray color of his skin was as well. The work was hard, and the hours endless. This pandemic had taken so much from so many, and never more than from frontline responders.

"I can't. I can't have this discussion with you. It's just a virus. Sure, a helluva deadly one, but the deaths are tapering off." He held up a hand defensively. "That isn't to discount the horror of it, the massive loss of life, so don't go there, okay? I'm just reluctant to announce that it is the end of humanity yet." Ander tried to smile. With his tired eyes and gray skin, it fell flat. "Humans are like cockroaches. We can survive anything and frequently do. Global warming. Climate change. The Collapse. All of it. And we rise again. Nothing keeps us down for long."

"This will, Ander. In the course of less than a year, we've seen over ninety-nine percent of our population die. This virus has eradicated entire blood types, entire populations of people." Beth persisted. "We are facing the existent possibility of the extinction of humanity."

Ander sighed. He opened his mouth, but at the moment the elevator doors slid open at the end of the hall, a gurney with a screaming pregnant woman and far too much blood for anyone's comfort came juddering out. Why she wasn't in the emergency room wasn't a question. They had time to ask. Ander was in motion, running as he directed the orderlies to an empty room nearby. The board lit up with a blinking call light for Room Six, sending Beth scurrying in the opposite direction.

It's no use talking to Ander about this. Or anyone else here at the hospital, for that matter.

Beth knew it was true. She needed proof, and she needed to talk to someone who understood genetics. If life had been different, if she could have afforded to continue her studies, she would have never have stopped at nursing. It had been merely a stopgap measure when the funding ran out and the bills mounted. She had hoped to return. To continue her studies, to dig deep into the study of genetics and modern human evolution. But she wasn't one of the luckier ones. Her grades were high, but not high enough. Her family wasn't well off, and loan caps, instituted mid-century as student debt soared to frighteningly high levels, had prevented her from continuing. The financial officer at school had been kind, but firm. Her grades weren't the highest, and the chances of her completing the course and finding a role in a crowded profession were slim. So nursing it was.

Dr. Brooks was so disappointed. She'd told me to keep trying, that my work was solid, but you can't keep going when there's no way to pay the tuition.

As she finished helping the woman in Room Six, whose twin daughters had passed in utero the day before and had to be delivered by cesarean section, her focus suddenly targeted her old teacher.

Dr. Brooks would know what to do. She might be gathering data on it now. Dr. Brooks had always focused on creating new, innovative changes in healthcare.

Later, in a quiet moment as the night slowly lost to the day, Beth typed up a note to her former instructor.

Transmission Packet

eenderman@mercynyhosp.edu to jbrooks@rutgers.edu

/BEGIN TRANSMISSION

Attended your Genetics and Humanity class in '97. Currently on staff in maternity ward at Grace in NY. Concerned about a sharp rise in miscarriage, fetal death/stillbirth, and neonatal death. Curious if you are researching the long-tail effects of the ESH virus in the reproductive-age surviving population.

/END TRANSMISSION

She pressed Send, stood up and stretched. Eight more hours to go. It was quiet now. Ander's shift had ended, and Voss and Anna had come in early. They looked well-rested after two full days off, practically chipper compared to the deep, abiding exhaustion Beth felt.

Outside, the sky had lightened, to deep reds and salmon pinks shot through with blues. In the distance, clouds formed, thick and dark.

"Weather's coming in. They think the tropical storm will resurrect and turn into a hurricane." Anna said, coming to stand by Beth's side. She was fresh out of nursing school. Anna experienced the baptism by fire when the ESH virus broke out and she saw it devastate the Big Apple. She'd asked Beth several times in the past few weeks if she needed a roommate. Even now, with more choices in housing, all rent free thanks to their now-vaunted status as medical personnel, it seemed the younger woman didn't want to live alone. Who could blame her, after all? It filled the city with corpses, and the empty streets were rather terrifying. Thanks to a lack of city engineers, the subway was likely permanently closed, and the rumors spread that New York itself might be closed down. Hadn't Ander mentioned it just the other day? That they were talking about building new cities, places free of corpses, decay, and ten billion rats, whose population, unlike humans, was rising exponentially.

"Giant 3D printers are creating buildings, streets, and more. The cities of the future." He had said.

Anna cleared her throat and Beth realized she had just stood there and said nothing in return to Anna's comment about the weather.

"A hurricane will swamp us, flood Manhattan, and the Bronx. I hear they are worried about the lower levels of the Met, and some of the public libraries too."

The sun lightened the sky, the brilliant colors of the sunrise faded even as the storm clouds grew. Far below, Beth could see trees swaying in the breeze. The last of their leaves flittered and flew through the crisp fall air, a carpet of orange, yellow and red covering the city streets. Beth tried to ignore the other things on the streets, notably a pack of rats the size of small dogs ambling along, as bold as you please.

In her pocket, her tablet buzzed with a notification. Beth reached for her tablet, keyed it on with her thumbprint, and read the message.

Transmission Packet

jbrooks@rutgers.edu to eenderman@mercynyhosp.edu

/BEGIN TRANSMISSION

Excellent timing, Beth. Good to hear from you. I'm currently reaching out to Dr. Julie Lynn Aaronson and hoping to assemble a team. Interested?

/END TRANSMISSION

Beth's heart gave a thump of excitement. Was she interested? Hell yes, she was! She wasn't sure what Dr. Brooks would want or need from her, but the idea of working with her former teacher, and that of the esteemed Julie Lynn Aaronson, well, she'd work sanitation if it meant spending her days in the two women's company. Her fingers flew as she fired back a response.

She finished the rest of her shift in a happy daze of excitement. Three more late-term fetal deaths before her shift ended tempered it. Also, the news that the woman in room 6, newly discharged from the hospital, had purposely stepped out onto the street in front of an autobus. This was quite a feat since the autobuses were all equipped with sensor technology that specifically scanned for pedestrians. As Beth passed a small crowd gathered on the sidewalk, she heard one of them say, "An autobus only requires six feet to stop. She walked out in front of it with less than two feet of clearance. You can't tell me she didn't see it."

Her heart sank. These deaths would continue. Not just the fetal deaths, but the others, like the woman in Room Six. What had her name been? Sarah? Sophie? She couldn't even remember now. Darkness closed in. Not just in the surrounding city, but in her chest, a mounting sense of dread. These deaths, these miscarriages, nothing like this had ever happened before. However, it felt as if this were just the beginning. She wanted to understand it. If they understood it, then perhaps they could stop it from happening. God, she would do anything to stop the pain she was seeing in others.

She hailed an autocar and went home to her tiny, lonely apartment, the memory of the sobbing mother holding her dead children echoing in her head.

Not Quite Human

05.01.2100
Fertility Research Institute

Syn Travani is a creche baby, one of the first batches born of no mother. *Genetically speaking, she is human, but her artificially sped up physical and mental development, her odd emotional responses, and her fiery eyes tell a different tale. Syn must navigate not just the normal trials and tribulations of growing up, but do it while being rejected by the very people who gave her life.*

"Hi Syn, how are you today?" The phlebotomist, a heavyset woman with short, curly gray hair, asked me. I had seen her before, we all had. Her name was Jane Wetzel. Her badge had tangled, reversed, so that her name didn't show, but here in this place, few things ever changed, and I knew all the staff by name.

I stare at her, unsure how to answer. Does anything change here, ever? Does she think I will feel differently today than I did yesterday? We built our existence on routine. Today is Wednesday, Blood Day as I like to call it. They always bring us to the lab on Wednesday and one by one, in the order of our age, which varies by minutes, hours, or days, we take turns sitting in the seat, watching. My eyes never stray as she wrapped the tubing around my arm, inserted the needle and three ampules of blood filled and removed. A cotton ball held in place by flexible bandage provides the adequate pressure to stop any further bleeding. I am fifth oldest, behind Hera, Lilith, Gaia, and Eve.

Monday had been Physical Day, Tuesday was Learning Assessment Day, and tomorrow will be Vision Test Day, Friday will be Psychological Assessment Day, and the weekends are when we will visit New Athens. I both love and hate the visits to the city. There are always interesting places to go, the zoo, the observatory, the gardens and parks. But everywhere we go, they stare at us. One glance at our eyes and they know. The murmuring begins, as do the curious stares. Or at worst, open hostility and even occasional muttered threats of violence. It worsens each time we undergo another maturation cycle.

She waits, a small smile on her lips, her brown eyes curious. She expects an answer, but I have none to give her. How am I? Better to ask *who* am I, something even I cannot quantify or answer. Doctor Mannis asked me that two weeks ago, I have yet to answer him, but he wrote copious notes despite my silence. Perhaps he did it to fill the silence with something, anything, beyond the sound of his own voice.

I say little. Honestly, I see no reason to do so, especially once I realized they found the silence uncomfortable. I suppose there is some measure of joy in staring at them in silence, letting them draw their own conclusions, their friendly tone slowly dropping away, the words leaving them, or speeding up. Some speak faster, fill the void with random noise. They cannot abide silence, none of them. I unhinged them with the ring of fire that surrounded my pupils, my lack of emotion and wordless stare.

I'm sure they find it a flaw in my character. I watch as they fill the chart with notes and labels.

She waits a second more, her gaze sliding away, the small smile dead and gone, a tight, forced one in its place. I resolve to smile at her next week. Perhaps I will even answer Doctor Mannis on Friday, or let the words tumble over themselves. I derive a tiny, perverse pleasure in being unpredictable.

She reaches for the tubing, wrapping it around my arm and instructs me to make a fist. I comply, watching as the red blood jets through the needle and tubing and into a small ampule.

"Four today, Syn," she says as she quickly switches them out. "I need it ahead of the next maturation cycle."

My face betrays a sliver of my discomfort. Another maturation cycle is approaching. They will sedate us. The effects of the massive amounts of changes are debilitating and painful. I remember nothing of the first cycle, though we later learned that our tiny bodies did nothing more than scream and writhe in our cribs until they put us under. My next memory was of waking up differently. I was taller, for one, and could nearly reach the light switches. Before that first cycle, I had barely learned to walk. After, I had stumbled about for weeks, tripping over bigger feet and legs, trapped in a body that was alien to me. It sticks in my memory, yet another difference between my kind and a normal human child. How odd to *not* remember the first few years of your life!

When it was time for the next maturation cycle, they explained we would sleep for a while and when we woke up, we would be different. And again, it was a shock, now I could easily reach a light switch, see the tops of counters, and, once I had adjusted to the longer legs, I ran faster than my creche-mates, my black hair streaming out behind me.

I have endured three maturation cycles, one each year, and each time emerged from two weeks of sedation in a body that has grown the equivalent of five years physically and mentally.

Her hands deftly switch out another ampule and she tries to smile again, "This will be the last one, Syn."

Does she reference the ampules? Three sit on the table, full. Or does she mean the maturation cycles? In a few more weeks, I will emerge fully grown, just in time for the fourth anniversary of my removal from the artificial womb. Their antiquated traditions of wishing each of us a happy birthday on the anniversary of our transition from amniotic fluid to an existence of breathing air seem odd. What is so special about it? Why should they care? Why should we? I don't mind the cake, however, a small individual one for each of us, baked to order according to our individual preferences. Last year I asked for a yellow one, with raspberry filling, chocolate frosting and bacon slices. I found it quite satisfying.

Still, I nod, remembering what Doctor Mannis has said about copying mannerisms to appear more acceptable to others. It is a pointless gesture. Jane Wetzel does not see it; she is looking down. I add a quiet mutter that sounds affirmative.

Fake it until you make it, Syn.

She looks up, her eyes steady on mine, one of the few willing to look me directly in the eye. If I were to like anyone, I think I would choose her. Her nature is one of acceptance and pragmatism.

"Does it frighten you?"

I cock my head. Yet another trick I learned from Doctor Mannis. It means that I don't quite understand the question. A simple head movement, but it asks a question, or at the least shows that more data is required before an answer can be given.

"Does the thought of undergoing the last maturation cycle make you nervous?"

I ponder this for a moment. "Should it?"

"I just think it must be hard to adjust to. You go to sleep and when you wake up, your body and mind have changed significantly. You are taller, and, er, more developed."

I nod. "Everything feels... *different.*"

She nods and squeezes my hand. Does she do this to reassure me? Does this mean I should smile? I comb through my experiences with her and the other medical staff, searching for the response. I don't like for her to touch me, but I have learned not to pull away. It reminds them of how different I am, how different we all are, my sisters and I.

She leans closer and I see her steal a glance at where the security camera is as she positions herself so that my body blocked the view of her mouth. She whispers then, "There are some of us who don't think this should continue, Syn, these experiments."

I don't react. What does she mean? I am an experiment. Does she wish to discontinue me? To stop the cycle of tests and questions and learning they tell us is so important?

"You are human, Syn, and these tests, these things they have done to you and your sisters in the name of science or the future of humanity, they aren't right."

I blink, confused. She darts a quick glance again at the camera in the room's corner. "We can help you get out of here. If you want to be free, we will help you."

I say nothing. I can't help thinking of how Dr. Aaronson and Dr. Brooks, the developers of the artificial wombs, had disappeared during our last maturation cycle. Before that time, they had been here every day. Dr. Aaronson had held my hand, still smaller than hers, and smiled at me reassuringly. Of all of my sisters, I have displayed the most emotion, especially that of fear, when faced with the changes that will come from another cycle. She had been the last thing I saw before my eyes slipped closed. The drugs that would keep me in a coma-like state flowing freely into my veins.

"I'll be here when you wake, Syn." But she hadn't been, and neither had Dr. Brooks. Someone told us they were no longer part of the project months later.

Do I want to be free? What would that mean?

She is waiting for an answer and I shake my head. She nods and then lets me go, saying cheerily, "All done, Syn, and off you go now. I hear they are serving something special for lunch. You won't want to miss it!"

I slip from the chair, stand up, and walk away without a glance. Her words have stirred something in me, but what exactly it is, I understand even less than she does. As I move down the corridor, I catalogue the things I know, the facts about myself. A list of bulleted points in my mind...

- My name is Syn Travani and I will be four years old in one month. My body is the developmental equivalent of a fifteen-year-old girl.

- I picked my name for myself at the end of my second year. Syn is short for synthetic. Travani was the character in a book I read on the 'net, a favorite of mine, *Travani and the Zoot Suit*.

- I am 1.75 meters tall and I weigh 60 kilos. My hair is black, my eyes are blue/shot with fiery streaks, like all the creche-born.

- I am the offspring of no single man or single woman. Instead, my body carries a blueprint of no less than six individual DNA profiles.

- I was not born. Releasing a valve on an artificial uterus is not the same as how human children typically come into the world. I prefer to think of it as hatched, although that is not accurate either.

- Although my genetics declare me human, the strangers on the street, along with my mind and body, scream that I am "other." What that otherness is, I cannot explain nor completely understand. And neither can the humans who surround me.

I mull these facts over as I move down the hall. Should I wish to be saved? Am I, as she said, truly human? Do I deserve something different from what I have? Will being "free," whatever that truly means, make me feel better somehow?

Freedom, as much as I understand it, is a right gifted to all law-abiding citizens of the Terran United Planetary Government. Am I a citizen? Would I break the law by leaving this facility where I have lived for nearly four years? And what would my life be outside of these walls?

In the end, the question was moot. The following Wednesday, she wasn't there. A different tech, whose badge identified her as Gigi Sanders, had taken her place. A new face. How unusual.

"Your name?" she asks, not looking up, not meeting my gaze. So many of them are like that. It is as if they fear seeing something there, something that will change them as irrevocably as it has changed us. As if I could infect her with my fiery gaze.

"Syn Travani," I reply, studying her. She is young, with mousy brown hair and brown eyes, what little I can see of them. A split second, she makes eye contact and then looks away, trying to appear busy with the task at hand. She retrieves her clipboard, makes a checkmark next to my name, and writes the identification number tattooed on my skin in the space on the paper.

"Sit down and hold your hand out."

I do as she instructs, taking the moment to study her as she ties the tubing around my arm, slides the needle into my skin, and the blood fills the vial.

"Where is Jane?" I ask her.

"Jane?"

"The phlebotomist that normally takes my blood."

"I don't know. Perhaps she was transferred?"

Or perhaps we were overheard. It isn't just cameras, after all. They heard her talking to me.

"I'm sure that is what it was."

"Do you have a question? Something I can help you with, Syn?" She asks it quickly, and there is something in her voice, overeagerness perhaps, that warns me off.

"No."

She nods, fills a second ampule, removes the needle and tubing and presses down on the crook of my arm with a thick cotton ball, affixing it in place with a flexible strip of bandage that wraps around my arm.

I say nothing more and leave when she is done with me.

The next day begins early, before the sun has risen. I have not slept. I can do this easily, for up to three days at a time before suffering any ill effects, but doing anything more than lying in my bed alerts them. Although I have never seen them, I am sure there are cameras in each of our rooms. They watch us even as we sleep.

The alarm next to my bed chimes at five a.m. It is melodic, not harsh, but I am already awake. I lay there unmoving since eleven, my eyes closed, my breathing slow and measured. I will sleep enough in the weeks to come.

"The last maturation cycle," the director said yesterday, his voice ringing across the cafeteria. We sat, our plates empty, and listened. "When you wake up, your bodies will have taken the last steps from adolescence to womanhood." He paused and his lips stretched into a creepy simulacrum of a smile. "You will emerge from it able to bear children and help save humanity from extinction."

I wondered if he expected us to applaud.

"You will have no higher duty, nor more sacred obligation, than to nurture the children of the future in your wombs."

And with those words, I thought of one area of study I had indulged in, Twenty-First Century Filmography, an elective, something I took simply to understand humans and their emotions better. One show stood out, one from the earlier decades of the century, *The Handmaid's Tale*. A popular dystopian tale which had been turned into a serialized television show. It followed the story of one woman, torn from her husband and child, subjugated, and forced to submit to ritualized rape in order to bear a child for a couple who were infertile.

After having studied the history of the Reformed United States of America, I couldn't help but imagine fiction becoming reality. Especially now, as I sat listening to the director.

The stated mission had changed. All of my life, they told us we were supposed to be the future of humanity in and of ourselves. Born of no single woman, our very existences are, in a sense, manufactured. The hopes of others being created this same way, generations upon generations if need be, had now changed and altered. It was the first any of us had heard of it and a quiet murmur rose at my table and others.

Bear children? For ourselves? For others? When had the mission changed? When had we become less than enough? Was it our eyes? Our limited emotions? Would they take our children and give them to barren couples? Were we simply an experiment to them, inhuman, yet human enough to bear the future generations of children for those whose wombs no longer functioned?

I mulled this over as I reported to the maturation chamber, clad in the thin shorts and halter top I would wear while my body and mind grew as I slept. It was the last thing I thought about as the sedatives rushed into my bloodstream and it was the first thing I thought of when I regained consciousness eighteen days later.

"Five centimeters taller, Syn." A nurse named Andrea said as she helped me onto the table. I was still woozy, still a mess of tangled limbs and cobwebs in my skull, my reflexes dulled by the drugs that had kept me under. I stunk, I lifted an arm and a wash of body odor hit me.

"I need to shower." My voice sounded rusty, like an old metal gate.

"Soon, Syn, we just need to finish a couple of tests."

This included a pelvic exam, pap smear, and more blood tests. I hid a smile at the thought of the nurse having to endure my body odor. She should have let me take a shower first. The grim set to her mouth betrayed her discomfort and a few minutes later, she helped me off the table.

"Here, eat a protein bar and drink some water before you leave. I don't want you passing out in the hallway or the shower."

I did as she asked and the dizziness cleared. "What day is it?"

"Tuesday, but don't worry about it. Today, and the rest of the week, are free days. Return to your room, shower, spend some time with your creche-mates, the Director will call an assembly tomorrow."

Our routine had been a constant in my daily life, and except for several holidays clustered around the end of the year, *nothing* ever changed. The concept of free time was unheard of. We were to keep ourselves busy, learning, exercising, and, of course, enduring constant testing. It was simply the way things were. For the first time it occurred to me that perhaps this was not normal, that the few children born the old-fashioned way, grown in their mother's wombs, that those children did not endure constant tests, assessments and training. Having an absence of it felt wrong, an ominous unknown. Change was coming. I could sense it.

They kept some pieces of our routine. At half-past eight, the lights flickered off and then on again. It was our five minute warning to prepare for bed. I shared a room with Eve, the second-eldest of our creche. As the lights turned off for good, her hand pointed towards a corner of the room and pressed a button on a small receiver nestled in her palm. For a brief instant, I saw a red dot appear in the same corner, betraying the location of the camera I had suspected was there. A few seconds passed and then she spoke in the darkness, "Changes are coming. Big ones."

Eve and I, despite sharing a room, barely spoke. Each of our creche had found interests in different areas. For me that had been art, for Eve it had been computers. And now, in the darkness, she explained how that could help us. "I learned how to hack into the mainframe two maturation cycles ago," she said, "And how to cover my tracks, as well as redirect the security camera and audio monitoring in this room."

"Okay."

"Their meeting will begin in twenty more minutes. They will discuss the failure of the program, and what their next steps will be. Would you like to listen to it?"

"Yes."

The moonlight streamed into our room through the window high on the wall. Outside of the reinforced glass were steel bars. I could see her smile then. Cast in moonlight, dappled with shadows, it appeared less like a smile and more like a grimace of pain. She pointed at the device again, her fingers moving over the keys.

The burst of sound a few minutes later made me flinch. For fifteen minutes we listened to chairs scraping, the door opening and closing, and snatches of conversation that described lives far different from this facility.

"*Dollars for Babies* is really gaining traction, nearly five million viewers according to the Nielson-Behring reports."

"I told Stan that we needed to bring in at least one more partner and become a triad. More chances for a successful pregnancy, but he wants to wait for the Reproductive Promotion Center to open up next year. I'm thirty-five. I don't have a year to wait!"

"You've run all the tests? All of them? You're *sure* they are infertile?" That voice was the Director's.

A click of the button and the room fell silent. Eve spoke into the darkness. "They meet each week. I've been listening to them for the past three months."

"I haven't heard this before," I say, confused. *How have I missed this?*

"I record them, then listen to them later with my earbuds jacked in to the cochlear implant."

"Oh."

A chime sounded and Eve pressed the button again, filling the room with the sound of fingers on keyboards and the Director's voice.

"We are all here, so let's get this meeting started. Noel, could you give us a rundown on the maturation cycle?"

I frowned in the darkness. I had never met a staff member named Noel.

Noel gave her report, describing our physical and mental maturation as complete. "They have become fully mature, and no further forced maturation is necessary. From our tests, we have determined that each girl is the equivalent, physically, of an eighteen-year-old human girl. The human brain continues to develop until our mid-twenties, however, each of them were already testing at age twenty or above in the decision-making and accountability sectors *before* the last maturation cycle. I fully expect that their mental maturity will be close to, if not exceeding, that of a normal twenty-five-year-old when we run a full battery of tests next week."

She then described our physical changes, noting that most of us had grown up to five centimeters in height, with variances of 1-2 centimeters across the board. As she neared the end of her report, the Director cut her off abruptly.

"Thank you, Noel. I will appreciate a report with the exact details and variances on my desk in the morning. Andrea, you have news for us on the FSH levels?"

Andrea was the nurse who had been there as the sedatives wore off and the one who had drawn my blood this morning.

"Yes," she sighed, "All readings on all the girls were over thirty mIU." A murmur swept through the room. "As you all know, anything over twenty-five mIU shows ovarian failure."

"Is this due to the accelerated growth rate?" a voice asked.

"Not from what we can tell. Obviously, we could not create this creche in an Unaffected Persons camp as they have remained violently opposed to any approach by ESH positive. For good reason, the ESH virus remains unchanged since it's last mutation. The incubation rate stands at eighteen to twenty days and is as lethal as ever."

"Goddamn Eco-Nu, damned if they didn't doom us all." Another voice muttered.

Eco-Nu was the company responsible for the bio-engineered virus that had killed over 99.6% of the world's population and left the survivors infertile. It had been nearly five years, and no amount of research by what it left of the world's greatest minds could crack it. The virus remained in nearly 100% of the population, except for a handful of surviving UPs, hidden in pockets around the world. And as infectious as it was, approaching them, interacting with them face to face, or even so much as touching the supplies they needed was akin to signing their death warrants.

In the last three years, someone had wiped three UP outposts out because of an accidental infection. And while several of the larger groups had agreed to move into the city currently being constructed by robots on San Miguel, an island off of the coast of California, they violently opposed any level of contact with the ESH positive population.

The murmurs had increased, and there were multiple conversations to follow, so much so that I had difficulty picking out the individual voices. The Director slammed his hand down on the table and demanded silence.

"So what we have produced in the past four years of experiments are a group of infertile four-year-old girls who *look* like they are adults and have the characteristic range of mild to moderately significant autistic behaviors. Have I got that right?" His voice was bitter.

Dr. Mannis, the psychiatrist, spoke up, "That pretty much sums up exactly the problem at hand. Worse, the general population remains under the opinion that the creche babies are not human. It has caused no small amount of criticism, verbal attacks, and even threats."

The Director spoke again, "So we can't integrate them into society. And they are useless to us as Breeders."

A woman's voice spoke then. She sounded familiar, but I struggled to identify who she might be. "Director, these girls are human and have rights."

"Oh please, Daria, spare us your sanctimonious lecture on souls and intangibles," another man snapped, "We created them in test tubes, you can't point to their parents, or even attribute a smile or a personality trait to a single one of the donor material we used. You sound like Aaronson and Brooks, and you see where that attitude got them."

"All I'm saying is that we cannot discard them. And they are not prepared for the world outside. They barely understand it!" Daria pressed, her voice breaking. "They are individuals, varied, unique."

"They are nothing of the sort. Not a single one has so much as an iota of feeling, compassion or connectedness. They barely speak. They are on level with a learning robot, just clothed in flesh instead of wires and plastic." His voice was harsh, dismissive.

Daria kept trying, "Doctor Mannis, what is your opinion on this?"

Dr. Mannis cleared his throat, "Well, I, hm..." he paused, as if searching for the words. "They all display strong learning abilities - retention of what they have learned, and..."

"Not a single iota of emotion," interjected the man.

"That isn't true!" Daria protested, "We haven't given them *love*. Instead, we have merely met their physical and educational needs. A child needs *love* to flourish!"

"Love won't make them fertile."

"Enough!" The Director's voice broke through the bickering. "Please continue, Doctor Mannis."

Dr. Mannis' tone was hesitant, "I think that, I mean, based on the tests I have performed, all subjects score incredibly low on the social interaction scale. There are some autistic behaviors, but the overarching problem here is that they are different and they know it. And they have seen others' reactions to them. It will not get better. I see developing behaviors, antisocial personality traits, that appear to be getting worse." He paused. "I think we need to ask ourselves why we would want more of these individuals in our future. If they cannot bear children, and they do not fit in with our surviving population, then we need to turn our focus to finding a place for them and ending this experiment. Artificial wombs are flawed. They cannot replicate what occurs in a human body. And if we quantify our humanity on the act of conception and gestation within a woman's body, then yes, I would have to agree. They are not human, and we have abundant proof of that over the past four years."

Eve hit the button on her device and the room fell silent, muting the conversation in the conference room on the other side of the complex. She said nothing, the room quiet, except for the sound of our breathing.

"We're nothing but failed experiments to them." Her voice came out of the dark, and I closed my eyes, a strange feeling of hurt and betrayal rushing over me. "And what does one do with failed experiments?"

"They wouldn't dare," I said in return. "How would they explain it away?"

"An accidental fire, explosion, maybe. Or perhaps they would just say that the ESH virus activated in us during the last maturation cycle and we died the same way nearly eleven billion others did." Her voice remained calm. "Death is part and parcel of this world. It would be nothing new to them."

"So we leave. Tonight."

"Yes."

"What about the others?"

She sat up, fully clothed. "Give me five minutes to set up the loops on the footage. Then we wake everyone, tell them what has happened, and give them a choice. Stay or go."

I sat up as well, pulling my nightshirt off of me in one quick movement. I reached for my clothes in the drawer beside me. "Do you think any will stay?"

Eve made a sound that was almost a laugh. "Stay and die, leave and possibly survive. I know what I'm choosing."

And half an hour later, while the disagreement was still raging in the conference room, with the Director shouting for the others to calm down, forty-two of us were moving down the hall to the emergency exit. Eve had disabled the alarms, creating a way out for us that didn't involve direct conflict with the facility guards, something I and others had insisted upon. They might not consider us human, but I wasn't willing to take the lives of innocent men in order to save my own.

Eight stayed behind. They all had their reasons. Ones they didn't share with the rest of us. They had thought it through. They had promised to buy us as much time as possible. And thankfully, the board had not made a decision that night. By the time they discovered we were missing, we had gained an eight-hour head start and melted into the mountains where there were no people, only abandoned towns and skeletal remains. We easily hacked the driverless cars thanks to Eve's skills, then dispersed far and wide. For me and my sisters, it was a simple task to disappear. Contact lenses concealed our fiery eyes, and I enlisted in a salvage crew outside of New York.

A few months after we left, a news report rolled in. I sat on the steps of the Met next to AJ, a wiry teenager with skin as black as tar while he read the article on his comlink.

Devastating Fire at Research Facility Kills Eight

A research facility in Arlington, Virginia was leveled after a late night explosion. The facility had been experimenting with artificial wombs as a way of circumventing the high number of miscarriages and in vitro deaths caused by the ESH virus. Fire investigators are sifting through the rubble to understand what caused the explosion and fire. Meanwhile, the renowned bio-geneticist team of Dr. Julie Lynn Aaronson and Dr. Janelle Brooks, in Genesis, Mississippi, are calling for a full investigation, claiming there are another forty-two other test subjects who are missing.

"Jesus, whatcha think of that, Cinderella?" No matter how many times I corrected him on my name, or its spelling, he ignored me and it had spread now to the rest of the team.

"I think it's time I went to Mississippi." I answered.

AJ laughed, then stopped and stared. "Wait, what?"

I smile and slap him on the knee. "Gotcha. But seriously, I gotta take some time off. The smell is getting to me. I'm gonna go check out one of the new cities and try to forget what two hundred million rotting corpses smell like."

It is the first lie I have ever uttered. I say it smoothly, with no hesitation. It is easier than I thought.

Sitting there at the Met, I realized for the first time who would help us. A call to Eve and she agreed. We might have gone our separate ways, but we kept in contact. Eve's abilities at hacking have got me the I.D. I needed to become a salvage worker that specializes in Renaissance art.

"Use the other I.D. I made you," she instructed, and I told her I would. For all we knew, there was a price on our heads and failed experiment or not, I had no interest in leaving this world soon.

Two days later, I'm in Genesis, Mississippi. Eve is at my side. She raised an eyebrow at my tats. I'd had AJ's cousin working on a full-sleeve tattoo on my right arm. It was still red and puffy in areas, the ink dark and new against my skin. A double helix wound its way around my arm. Closer inspection showed the DNA strands to be computer cables, with network cards and miniature hubs woven in.

Her only comment was, "Human, not quite human. Could you be more obvious?"

She dyed her hair brown, her clothes fashionable yet utterly forgettable, and she had chosen contacts that turned her eyes a muddy brown. In contrast, my head was shaved on one side and braided on the other, streaks of purple running through the black.

"I can see you've chosen the hide in plain sight approach." Her mouth twisted into a frown.

I let her disapproval roll off of me. Her way was not my way, and I was far safer with my tattoos and half-shaved head than she was in her conforming outfit. In New York, no one gave a shit what you looked like. "Next time you see me, I'll have the other arm done, too."

Her lips pursed in disapproval. "Let's get this over with. I've got a flight in two hours."

I nodded, and side by side, we walked into the lab complex.

ONE HOUR LATER

"I think you are going to miss your flight." The bench was cold and the handcuff that connected me to Eve through a steel base built into the bench was uncomfortably tight.

"Perhaps."

She was as emotionless and unruffled as ever. A few months in the bigger world, and Eve seemed the same.

In comparison, I felt as if I had become someone new. Perhaps it was the job I was working on, a section of the Met that focused on art from the early to mid-21st century. The fact was, I had fallen in love. Head over heels for a painter, if such things were possible, and a dead painter at that. Her canvases spoke a language of their own, filled with heartache and longing. Or perhaps that was my interpretation of it. The Met held four of them, two secreted away, moved to a safer place than the stone and glass edifice. It wouldn't be long before floodwaters lapped at, then took over, the tangled monstrosity of buildings expanded and built over for over two hundred years. My job was to help empty it, to clear its corridors of priceless works of art from every century of the past two millennia.

The artist's signature, small, precise - CLPA - a woman who didn't wish to abandon her maiden name and wrote it fully on the back of each canvas once she had finished. It had, according to the records, been one of her first. The placard on the wall told a tale of a young wife and artist, ready to build a life with her new husband, to raise a house filled with the laughter of children, and instead losing her dreams to a painfully premature birth. I had looked her up, this Carrie Lynn Perdue Aaronson. She signed her name on the back of the canvas in a flowing script that was a study in contrasts to the simple signature on the front. That and the date. According to the biography, her lost child would be a doddering grandmother by now had she survived.

For all I knew, this artist and Dr. Aaronson might even be related somehow.

A biography, written by her sister-in-law Jessica Aaronson Farnsworth, had detailed Carrie's life, as well as her paintings. I had found the book online and read it. Despite the decades, the gulf between her world and mine, I could feel her pain, her agony, and the struggle to bring life into the world. Call it coming to terms with it all, but the realization that I could *never, ever* hope to have a child of my own made me suddenly, inexplicably want one. Just a flash of longing, really. The thought was ridiculous, I was neck deep in a rotting city where the rodents outnumbered humans a million to one. I had barely lived my life, and wasn't ready for parenthood anymore than I was looking for a man, or woman, to spend my life with.

But I looked at Carrie's paintings and longed for something I never dreamed of wanting.

"Earth to Syn."

Eve's voice interrupted my ruminations, waving a hand in front of my face. She was standing, facing me, and her hands were free.

"How the..."

She shook her head, "While you've been saving art, if that's what you would call it, I've been learning new skills. Now, quick, before they come back to question us. It's time for Plan B."

I followed her down an empty corridor, at her heels as she moved across a hall into a half-empty room cluttered with boxes in one corner. We could hear footsteps down the hall.

"I wasn't aware of a Plan A, much less a Plan B," I whispered. The footsteps passed the room we were hiding in and continued on down the hall.

"Plan A didn't go so well with you looking tattooed and crazy. Or have you already forgotten how you decked the guy just because he wouldn't let you just waltz in and see Dr. Aaronson and Dr. Brooks?"

I grinned at her, "It got us in the facility, didn't it?"

Eve made a curious sound. It sounded like a strangled laugh.

"So where are they from here?"

"Two floors up."

"We could try the ventilation, it's big enough to hold us." I suggested, eying the large vent near the bottom of one wall.

"Or you could just use the elevator," the woman's voice at the door caused us to both jump. Her gray hair was pulled back in a bun, but the wisps flew in all directions, a halo of stray hairs surrounding what had started off as a neat coil of hair. The door, which we had closed behind us, was now open. Behind Dr. Aaronson were the two security officers who had detained us after I punched their obtuse co-worker.

Before either of us could react, she moved into the room, her hands held up in front of her, a familiar smile on her face, "You are safe here, truly you are, and I am so relieved to see you both."

Eve stood up first, dusting herself off before reaching out a hand to Dr. Aaronson. The guards tensed and one moved a step forward. Dr. Aaronson grasped Eve's hand inside of both of her own. Her eyes traveled over first Eve and then me.

"Just one year, and I see so many changes in you." Her gaze fell on my tattoo and moved to my half-shaved, half-purple head of hair. Her mouth quirked up at one corner. "Ah Syn, I expected nothing less, you showed an independent streak early on when you shaved the heads off of all the dolls. Do you remember that?"

I nodded, suddenly overwhelmed by emotions I didn't understand. Of all of the medical staff, she had been one of the few I cared for. Perhaps it was her tone, warm, and direct. Or the way she would answer questions, without obfuscation or delay. If I was human at all, it was in her eyes. Coming here had been the right choice after all.

A short walk down the hall, and a lightning fast ride on the elevator and I watched as Dr. Aaronson used a key and password combination to enable us all access. Good news, it required a key and number combination which I had easily memorized and which hopefully no one from the facility in Arlington knew about. Bad news, well, it was only bad news if we were indeed locked in with no way to leave.

Doctor Aaronson must have sensed our concern, she turned to us and smiled as we all moved onto the shining white floor, "You are safe here and you may leave whenever you wish. No harm will come to you." She said it as she nodded to the security, "Your presence is no longer required. And if anyone asks after them, I will remind you that I report directly to Chairwoman Chen."

The men nodded, returned to the elevator and disappeared behind the smooth metal doors.

"You found them!" Dr. Brooks rounded a corner, pulling off gloves as she hugged first Eve and then me in turn. It was disconcerting, touch was something we were still unused to. She held me at arm's length then, her eyes running the entire length of me, pausing as Doctor Aaronson had on my tattoo and hair before grinning, "You have to be Syn. The hair is a dead giveaway." She turned away, stared at Eve for a moment and asked, "And you, my dear, I'm not as good at faces as Julie is, but I'm going with Eve. Are you Eve?"

Eve nodded, no trace of emotion.

"And your sisters? Are they well?" Dr. Aaronson asked.

"All but the eight that stayed behind, yes, as far as I know." Eve answered, "Some chose to cut all ties and disappear. Not a bad decision when you consider what happened to the ones who stayed."

"Yes, indeed." Julie Aaronson's face turned dark with anger, "First ousting us from the research and then assuming we would say nothing about their mysterious fire."

"You were removed from the project. Why?" Eve went straight to the point, "One day you were there, the next you weren't."

The two women looked at each other, a silent exchange.

"We had different interpretations of what success looks like," Dr. Brooks said dryly, "The artificial wombs worked, just not in the way that others had hoped."

"Not in the way you hoped either." Eve said it, her face expressionless, "It's not as if we are human - not in their eyes, and not even in yours."

"That's not true, Eve, not at all!" Doctor Aaronson half rose from her seat, her face flushing. "Every bit of you is human, down to the last molecule, don't let anyone tell you differently."

Too many already had, though. From the sideways glances on the outings to the new cities, or the way that the research team member's eyes had slid across us, deliberately avoiding our eyes. Daughters of no single man or woman, grown in a nutrient bath inside an artificial amniotic sac until a pre-set hatching date - we were unique, odd, and intellectually and physically advanced - but we weren't quite human. We lacked the lifeline, the umbilicus and a living, breathing mother could have given us. The tattered remnants of the Catholic church had denounced us as abominations, as accursed. We weren't human, no matter what the DNA said.

"We need you to contact the others, find them, and bring them here." Dr. Brooks interjected into the silence that stretched out after Dr. Aaronson's words.

"No."

She blinked, "No?"

"No more experiments. No more tests. We are done being guinea pigs." Eve said, her voice hard and cold. "It's what we came to tell you."

The two scientists exchanged glances again, Dr. Brooks shaking her head, a rueful smile on her face. "You called it, love, as always."

"We just want to know," I added, "that we won't have targets on our backs. They might have it in their heads we are a threat, that we will cause trouble, but all we want is our lives. We want to live, secretly if need be, but without trouble, without injections and blood draws and tests every day."

"We want to be *free*." Eve added.

Both women nodded and Dr. Aaronson put her hand on my arm, her fingers settling on the tattoo and its strands of DNA woven from machine parts in stark black ink.

"You deserved better, Syn. You all did. We hoped the artificial wombs would save us, allow us a chance to ensure future generations of humans. You and your sisters proved that the wombs worked. I know that, with time, we can work out the kinks, but not at the expense of human lives. I will speak to Madame Chairwoman Chen herself and see that you are all free to live within our world."

She paused, then looked into my eyes, "We can reverse the high FSH levels. Janelle and I, we have been going over the reports from your last maturation cycle. We have allies, not everyone was happy with the board removing us from the program, and they have continued to update us with the latest information. Well, at least until the board shut it all down. Having children, it's not out of the question, Syn. If you want one, that is."

I shook my head, turning away from her. A child? Me? All I wanted was to return to the ruins of New York and sit there in the Met and imagine what it would be like to create art. I wanted to hold sculptures and peer at old photographs and surround myself with things that could not hurt me. If every last human were to disappear, I would be free to live in peace. No fear, no judgment, no questioning glances.

They let us go. And we walked through the group of restless, uneasy guards, feeling their eyes on our backs. We parted ways, Eve making a later flight than expected, disappearing into a crowd seamlessly, already at home with her anonymity. And I returned to New York. Back to the Met, back to a sea of art tampered only by the smell of rot that seeped through the buildings, filling the subways and streets with a sodden, off-putting pungency of decay. The city, still home to thousands, was dead. I moved into a high-rise. There was no electricity and the walk up to the 30th floor each evening ensured I had no neighbors, no curious eyes.

Thirty floors, two flights per floor, twelve steps each flight. By the end, my heart hammered in my ears. But the silence, with only my jagged breath to interrupt it, was payment enough. The apartment was spacious, open and minimalist and filled with a breathtaking view of the Hudson.

I tried to imagine what this world had looked like before the plague. In truth, I found it overly full of humans *now*. As the sun set, and the rays of red and burnt orange filled the floor to ceiling windows with a mix of shadow and light. For now, this was home. And for now, I was safe.

I dug into my rucksack and pulled out a hunk of cheese, along with an apple I had picked in the park. I sat cross-legged in front of the massive window, the concrete floor cool and smooth beneath me, ate my dinner and remembered how it had felt to have Dr. Aaronson's hand on my arm. She had been kind, gentle. Not all of them were bad. She would keep her word, I knew it. I closed my eyes then, savoring the flavors of the cheese and the apple as they mixed in my mouth.

I was free.

First Words

Date: 07.12.2101
Mars Year 15, Day 387
Huygens Outpost, Mars

"Seriously, Lenny, you are gonna break that thing." Nix groaned over the pile of bunting sitting next to the 3D printer.

"Toya wants…"

"Don't even get me started on what my dear wife wants. You would think it was a national holiday, Huan turning one Martian year old. Her and her talk of new traditions. I swear, she's sleep-deprived as hell and spreading it far and wide." Nix grumped, his fingers shuffling through the piles of bunting. "What in the hell are we gonna do with all of this after the party?"

Lenny grinned at his brother-in-law. "It's biodegradable and edible. The goats will love it. Promise."

Nix snorted and rubbed his eyes. "I'm so damned tired, I can barely think." And he was. Selena was three months old and showed absolutely no signs of conforming to any schedule whatsoever. She slept when she wanted, woke at all hours, and Nix, with zero experience in babies, was convinced he would never sleep for longer than two hours at a time again.

"Had you up at midnight again?" Lenny asked, pressing the button on the 3D printer to request another pile of bunting. The machine groaned and Nix couldn't help but commiserate.

"Midnight? Hell, I'd be so lucky if it was only that. Midnight, one, three, and at four-thirty she started on a defecation cycle that has to have produced more shit than I am capable of in a day. I truly do not know how she does it." He yawned. "And your sister, she sleeps through it all. Sleeps like the dead. I'd have told her where to stuff it when she asked me to help out but she's breastfeeding her as we speak. And that's something I don't have the equipment for."

Lenny stared at Nix's chest, looking thoughtful. "You know, the nanites could..."

"Don't even think of it."

Lenny smirked, "Right. No nanites for you."

Nix shook his head at the teen and scooped up the bunting. "So, where the hell is all this going?"

"Cafeteria."

Nix grumbled as he left, his arms overflowing with the bunting, still warm from the printer, "How many damned cafeterias is this supposed to fill, anyway?"

The delectable smells filled the hall long before he arrived at the cafeteria. Despite his exhaustion, Nix grinned. Abdul was at it again. He had become their de facto chef and organizer of all things social, something that each of the survivors found endearing about the small, quiet Middle Eastern man. He hadn't been content with honoring his beliefs, but incorporated as many of Earth's time-honored traditions as possible, whether or not there were representatives of the faiths or nationalities to justify it.

His efforts, however, were not unappreciated. Abdul had recently done a deep exploration of Scottish traditions and meals. This had included a sacrifice of one of the small herd of sheep they had been raising. The first generation, grown in the artificial wombs, had produced not just a second generation, but now, a third. With enough to spare, Abdul had diligently carved up the two-year-old sheep and created some monstrosity known as haggis. Had Nix *not* known what was in the haggis, he might have been able to eat it easier. However, he unwisely launched into a vivid description of how haggis is comprised of the heart, liver, lungs, and intestines. The taste of it, mixed with onions from the garden, and oatmeals from their extensive food stores, had been exotic to Nix's tongue. The realization he was eating intestines, however, made his stomach flop.

It had also convinced Abdul that it was in his best interest to *not* detail every ingredient, but simply gloss over some of the finer points that might set the others off their feed.

In the end, Toya, with an iron stomach and the rabid, postpartum hunger for nutrients while feeding Selena, hadn't cared a whit for what was in the haggis. She had tucked into it with gusto.

Right now, the smell of five-spice hung in the air. Abdul had promised to create some traditional Chinese dishes and Liu had looked pleased when their chef-in-residence had mentioned "long noodles" and "red eggs." Nix hoped that the birthday celebration also meant Kung Pao Chicken or Sweet and Sour Pork along with birthday cake. His stomach grumbled with longing the closer he drew to the cafeteria. The party was a couple of hours away, but he hoped Abdul would take pity on him and toss some fried rice his way. A man could get a lot done with a generous bowl full of Abdul's chicken fried rice.

Hours later, their group gathered in the cafeteria, all nine of them. Nix thought of the lifeships that would soon arrive and roost on the surface of Mars for the next decade or longer. The Philadelphia Hab contained only nine souls in a Hab built for two hundred or more. The halls held an echo of sorts, something halfway between death and loneliness, and he looked forward to seeing scores of others again. They got along well these days, but it would be nice to not know every painfully insignificant detail about another person again. His world was far too small.

They had waited until mid-afternoon for the party and Selena was wide awake, her eyes bright with curiosity. Toya held her up so she could see the birthday cake as it was being cut. Her tiny rosebud mouth was open in an "o" of what appeared to be excitement and interest. Nix hadn't really known what to expect from parenthood. He hadn't been around babies, or really ever thought he would be a dad, but Selena captivated him. She was far more interesting than they had led him to expect babies would be. In the depths of night, when the outpost was quiet and even the animals in Eden Hab slept, he would walk with her through the halls of the Hab and stare into her eyes. He could sense so much going on there. She might not have much to say yet, but he could tell that would change. He could see the gears whirring, as she took everything in - her surroundings, conversations, and so much more. He couldn't wait to share this world and others with her. As the project Petra had named Green Mars progressed, he dreamed of a day when his child would run outside, breathing Martian air and digging in the dirt without a dome in place.

Suddenly, in the lull of conversation as they all dug into the cake, Nix heard his daughter say, "shēngr" kuàilè!" as clear as a bell.

Liu's head snapped towards the baby, nearly dropping his fork. He stared at Selena in shock.

"She... she knows Mandarin? She is, she is so very young!"

Nix frowned, unable to see the look on Toya's face, since she faced away. "Did she say something in Mandarin? Actual words?"

Liu nodded, eyes transfixed, mouth hanging open. Nix noticed an errant dab of icing on his chin. "She said 'Happy Birthday' in Mandarin. I did not think a baby this young could, how you say," his mouth screwed up around and elongated the word, "*physically* form words."

"She shouldn't be able to. Infants' face, mouth and throat muscles haven't developed enough yet to produce speech," Toya replied after a long pause. She turned to Nix, eyebrows raised in question.

Nix shrugged, mystified. "She has said nothing in Mandarin that I know of." He picked up his fork, dug into the cake. "Just the standard English words."

"Wait, what?" Toya stared at him. "What 'standard English words?'"

He swallowed the bite of cake. It was delicious. Moist and full of flavor, better than he remembered. "Um, you know, the usual. 'Hi, bye, hungry, tired, mommy, daddy, go' - you know all the normal stuff." He took another bite of cake and looked up.

Now everyone was staring at him. Even Toya.

"Michael, are you saying our daughter says words out loud to you, at three months of age?" The expression on Toya's face made him nervous. What could he have done this time?

"Um, yes?"

"Holy shit, sis." Lenny barked with laughter. "Mom said you spoke for the first time when you were ten months, same as me. Full sentences by eighteen months. Selena's got us beat. Hands down."

Petra whistled. "Seriously? You all make me feel slow. And I was reading by the age of three!"

Lenny nodded. "Age two for me. And Toya beat me at that by a few months, according to our mom." He puffed out his chest. "She called us her wunderkind."

Nix wondered if he was being dense. "So, this isn't normal?"

Petra snorted, "God, no. It's got to be the nanites. Normal age for first words is around nine to twelve months, short sentences at age two to three years. And like you said, physically she shouldn't be capable of it."

Her eyes gleamed in interest then.

"Perhaps we could run some tests." Petra suggested.

"No." The answer was clear, definitive, and mutual, Toya and Nix speaking at the same time.

Petra raised her hands as if trying to placate Nix and Toya. "Nothing invasive. Just some basic tests that Mensa designed a few years back." She shrugged. "I mean, it would be a good idea to run a blood test to see if there are any residual nanites."

Nix could see Toya's hackles were up. Her lips had tightened into a thin line and her jaw clenched. "I said, 'no.'"

"Right. Got it." Petra's smile was strained. She reached for her plate and dug in, giving Nix a look that told him the argument was far from over. It was one drawback of living and working with a group of scientists. They were curious creatures and far more persistent than most. Petra wouldn't let this go and Toya remembered all too well the arrogance and disdain she had experienced before the nanites had fixed her damaged mind back to its original brilliance. She knew enough about Petra to know it had come from a place, as such things so often do, rooted in family trauma and competitiveness. Petra had wanted Nix. Nix had chosen Toya long before Lenny could create the nanites and design them to fix Toya's damaged brain. He had chosen a brain-damaged girl over Petra's formidable intellect, and that had rankled plenty.

Nix wanted to believe they had gotten past it, moved on. Hell, maybe grew a little. But he was stuck between two brilliant women, both scientists who possessed intimidating intellects. All Nix wanted was peace. He was equally certain that he would not get it.

Blink and We Might Miss It

The peace lasted for two days. It surprised Nix that it lasted that long. Two days after Huan's birthday party, Petra began dropping by when Toya wasn't around. Selena's sleeping habits abruptly leveled out, and she would wake only once each night to breastfeed. It was a relief to both Nix and Toya, especially with the workloads they were carrying.

Toya was deeply involved in the Lazarus project, which included producing an army of bots to construct the fields of solar arrays the hundreds of thousands of Cryo units would need to remain powered on Mars.

Nix was equally busy on Eden Hab, which was flourishing, but still needed hours upon hours of work to transform the rest of the regolith into viable soil. The areas where they had laid the hundreds dead were verdant, thanks to amendments that transformed the corpses into a nutritive soup, which fed crops for the livestock. The flock of geese was new, as were the two calves, Guernsey and Bonnie Bell. In a few more months, they would be mature enough for the first round of in-vitro fertilization. By the time the first of the lifeships arrived, the first Martian-born cows not grown in artificial wombs would roam a section of Eden Hab. The goats and sheep had their own pens, and the chickens roamed freely. Nix regularly chased down Bellatrix, a black-feathered Svart Hona hen who loved to hang out near the airlock and run through when he least suspected it.

It was easy enough to bring Selena along with him to Eden Hab. The infant would stare out from her snug baby wrap positioned against his chest, her eyes tracking the animals, the plants, everything. Hours after the party, she had spoken to Toya for the first time, which had abated the accusatory stares Nix had been receiving. He wondered if she was upset that Selena had only said words around him first.

Likely she talked to me first because Toya has just known *what Selena needs from the get go. I'm smarter than the average bear, but compared to Toya, I'm the slow one here. I need all the verbal cues I can get.*

The question of what the nanites might have done to a developing fetus was certainly on his mind, and likely everyone else's. It was an unknown. When Lenny had injected the nanites into Toya, no one had known she was pregnant. And the nanites, charged with a mission to head straight for the brain, had done their job. They had simply headed for both Toya's brain *and* the tiny fetal brain growing inside of her uterus.

No matter how they looked at it, Selena was the first of her kind. A child born not only of one parent with dizzying intellect, and the other of above average intelligence, but all of it augmented by the as yet unquantified power of the nanites. Trained to find damage and repair it. What had they done in Selena's developing brain? Would they consider it something in need of repair or improvement?

Nix mused on it as he worked through the various paddocks, tidying, feeding, watering. Bellatrix had made a break for it, but upon bringing her back, Nix had discovered a nest nestled on the edge of a compost heap, six eggs filling it. He candled one and grinned. The rooster had done his job, too. It looked like the eggs were fertile. A couple more weeks and they would have chicks running about. The fifth batch in as many months. Petra's voice interrupted his dreams of the green paradise he was creating in Eden Hab.

"Morning, Nix."

He sighed. There was only one reason Petra was here. She hated the earthy smell of Eden Hab and said it reminded her of visiting a farm as a schoolgirl. She had slipped and fallen in a cow patty and ridden home, miserable and stinking, while the other children laughed. That was the reasoning she gave for not visiting it more often. But Nix suspected it had more to do with the bodies of the colonists, dead of the ESH virus, that lay beneath the surface of the regolith. Lenny had been right to suggest it, despite how off-putting it was to deal with the dead in this manner. Petra had hated every minute of the terrible process. Retrieving the bodies from outside of airlocks, removing their clothing, and burying them beneath the regolith. She had refused to go anywhere near Eden Hab for months afterward. The woman cultivated a stony exterior, but from their short time as lovers, he had caught glimpses of the fragile, traumatized woman underneath. She'd certainly hidden it well, but it was there.

"Petra." He glanced down at Selena. She had been dozing, but now opened her eyes, likely woken by the voices.

"I'm here to get some blood samples." Petra said, staring at Selena. Straight to the point, as usual. She had no patience for niceties and she certainly did not waste words.

"No." Nix knew the only way to deal with her was to be just as abrupt and succinct. It was the language she understood, after all.

Petra frowned, her lips pinched together. "Don't be a fool. We need to know what is happening inside of that baby. For research alone, it..."

"Her name is Selena, Petra."

"I know that."

"She is not 'that baby.' She is my daughter, Toya's daughter, and we will decide when it is time to take blood tests."

Petra stiffened, her jaw tightening. Nix watched as she breathed in, released it, and calmed the snarl forming there. "Toya and Lenny are working with Earth on the nanite technology. To hand over this technological advance without first knowing what exactly it has done to that..." she grimaced, and again stood silent for a moment before she continued.

"Nix, we need to know exactly what changes the nanites made to Selena. You know we need to. Blood tests. We need to gauge her IQ level, determine how many words she can speak, and how many she knows. We cannot in good conscience hand over technology that could alter people in ways we don't understand without first attempting to mitigate the risks."

Nix watched Petra as she stared at Selena. The infant stared back. He had spent the past 48 hours learning infant milestones and from what he could tell, no babies spoke, not at all, not for the first nine months of life, or more. Nix had been so busy getting used to the demands of this tiny creature, so full of work and exhaustion and more, that he truly had not known her talking was unusual. He felt foolish now. Embarrassed. All around him were intellectual giants. Even the smallest of them.

For a brief second, a flash of something else crossed her face. A millisecond and then it was gone. Was it longing he had seen there? Desire? Loneliness?

Petra had never struck him as maternal. In fact, truth be told, he didn't think she even wanted children. Seeing her staring at Selena, however, eroded that belief quickly.

Between the ESH virus, the massive asteroid heading towards Earth, and our own hubris, humanity is on the cusp of extinction. And hormones are powerful things. The drive for us to reproduce, to create life and fight the void. It is stronger than we might think. We like to believe we have evolved. But have we really? Or are we just monkeys with bigger, faster tools?

"Toya will have my balls if I let you poke and prod Selena." He finally said. "And between you and me, I prefer my balls intact. I will, however, speak with her about it." Petra opened her mouth as if she were about to object, but he didn't give her the chance. "You *will* wait on this, Petra. Nothing will happen in the next day or two, or even a week. Earth is too busy chasing their tails with the two lifeships departing from orbit in the next month. The scientists aren't even talking about the ESH virus or the teratogenic effects of it on fetuses right now. They have bigger problems, like making sure mass-produced Cryo units don't mean an exponential increase in the failure rate a handful of years from now. I'll talk to her. About the blood tests, the evaluations, everything. She will come around, but you have to take it slow."

Petra clenched her hands for a moment, her neck muscles corded, taut. Just like Toya, Petra enjoyed being in charge. So had Brigid Teraby, and Sonia Alouet, both long dead now. He seemed to attract brilliant, impulsive, control freak lovers.

You are the common denominator, Nix.

"Fine." Petra spat and turned on her heel.

"What? You don't want to stick around? I could use a hand mucking out the goat pen and the chickens need water."

Petra strode away from him toward the airlock. "It stinks of shit in here."

He watched as she opened the airlock and swore as Bellatrix darted between her legs, determined to find greener pastures in the innards of Philly Hab.

"Nix! The damned bird!" Nix swallowed his laughter and ran to catch up. The last time Bellatrix had given them the slip she had made it to Receiving. He'd found her perched on Sonia's old desk, puffing out her feathers. This time, he was quick enough. A dozen paces down the tube leading to Philly Hab and Bellatrix warbled in distress as he plucked her from the ground and turned on his heel, marching back toward the airlock. From her position in the wrap on his chest, just as he was passing Petra, Selena's little voice piped up.

"Bad bird!"

Petra gasped, her eyes widening.

"Nix!"

He didn't stop. "Yeah, yeah, I'll talk to her, Petra!"

Twenty minutes later, Toya was pacing back and forth, Bellatrix occasionally chasing after her each time she turned toward the chicken coop. Likely, the bird was looking for a treat. She was fuming. Worse, she wasn't saying anything. This was a sure sign of trouble.

Pre-nanite Toya would have simply accepted Petra's intrusion into their lives, but her newly regained intellectual prowess, combined with the fierceness that comes with new motherhood, had changed her. Nix was both supportive and slightly intimidated by the new Toya. He had worried at first that regaining her brilliant mind would dim her interest in him. He couldn't keep up with her. Even as a card-carrying member of Mensa in his own right. When she had woken up from the nanite treatment, he had backed away at first, unsure of whether their relationship would survive her return to herself.

The nanites were the key to everything. They had circled about inside Toya's brain, as well as Selena's. Yes, they had all evacuated upon command, but their effects on *Toya* were still being discovered. And now they needed to understand Selena, and gauge her development, before they released the nanite technology on Earth's citizens. To not fully understand *what* these nanites could do to the unborn, how the technology might affect the developing brain, would be irresponsible. And that is what he had to make Toya understand. It wasn't just needles and tests and subjecting their infant daughter to them both; it was being responsible for what came next.

Toya suddenly stopped pacing and eyed him balefully. "Fine. But why does it have to be *her*?"

Nix blinked in confusion. "Selena?"

"No." Toya's lips thinned. "Why does it have to be Petra who does the testing?"

"Well, as unbelievable as it might seem, she minored in child development and psychology. She's the closest thing we have to a specialist. And no," he said, seeing the look on Toya's face, "we can't wait for the lifeships. They are two years or more away. We need to study this now, and you know that as well as I do."

Petra had not been kind to Toya. And where she would have endured Petra's taunts before. Now she had only her memories of how Petra had talked down to her. She would no longer tolerate Petra's needling. And who could blame her? Nix felt the same way. Having Petra poke and prod their child was not something that either of them wanted, but it was necessary.

"Telegraphic speech, Toya. At three months." He bent his head to look at their child, sound asleep. Her tiny lips parted as her chest rose and fell. How he loved her, and the woman who had brought her into the world. He had wondered if he would ever have children, ever find someone he could be himself with. Toya had been that person, then and now. His voice softened.

"She is beyond amazing. And I wouldn't trade her, or you, for the world. But we have to understand this, log it, quantify it, and adequately prepare the rest of humanity for it. It could change everything we understand about human development. She's changing every day, Toya. Blink and we might miss it."

Toya sighed, his words, the way he held their child so close, the love he showed. It softened her expression.

"I know. But I want to be there, every step of the way. Let me have that, and I'll agree to it."

Nix nodded. He would make sure Petra was on her best behavior and that Toya was as well. They could, and would, work together to understand how the nanites had affected Selena, and what it might mean for humanity.

Only Time Will Tell

With Toya and Nix's permission, and a break in her schedule, Petra spent the next two weeks with Toya, Selena, and, as often as possible, Nix. The unspoken truce between the two women was a tentative thing, but slowly, Toya seemed less ferocious in her protectiveness of Selena. This was helped by Petra's unexpected patience and kindness toward Selena. Something that surprised Nix, who wouldn't have pegged Petra for the maternal type, not at all. Perhaps the ESH virus had changed that for all of them. Perhaps it had reset them all to a survival of the species mode.

Nix remembered some research he had read in college. *To be successful as a species, the members of that species must have a desire to survive long enough to pass on their genes to offspring. A species with a death-wish dies out rather quickly. Those species that don't die out have members that have devoted some attention to staying alive long enough to have young. It is from those individuals, and therefore, species that all living things are descended.* Perhaps the key to their survival, that of reproduction, had suddenly surpassed the priorities so lauded by their technologically advanced society. Nix suspected Petra had gotten the message early and often. Either choose a life of science and work, or choose ignorance and reproduction. It seemed very either or, and not much in between. He had seen Toya struggle with it. She wanted to be a mother and hold and love Selena, but she also clearly wanted to follow intellectual pursuits.

Why is it always either or? Nix mused. He thought of Abdul, who had embraced his role as their group's lead chef and cultural coordinator. Nix had learned more in the past year about Earth's customs and cultural interests than he had in over three decades of existence. That had to count for something.

He sat quietly in a corner of one of the Habs, taking notes for the further expansion of Eden Hab on his tablet as Selena slept in her makeshift bassinet. Petra and Toya reviewed the latest blood tests. Working together as peers, as scientists, the two women's formerly acrimonious relationship turned on its ear. Nix could tell that Toya was still waiting for the other shoe to fall and for Petra to turn, like a snake, and attack. She wasn't, however, and he suspected Petra had a change of heart.

"Only time will tell," Toya's words brought him back to the present. She and Petra were moving about the lab, tidying up.

"Indeed." Petra glanced over at Selena, fast asleep. She glanced up at Nix, her expression shifting from what he could only interpret as longing or regret to her standard, guarded look. "We're done. For now, at least." She glanced back at Toya. "We've established follow-up evaluations on a monthly basis for the rest of her first Martian year. That will give us a good baseline to report on what kind of affect nanites can have on the unborn." She stared again at Selena. "So far, your daughter has the verbal acuity of a two-year-old and the mental capacity of a two-year-old. Her physical development, while significantly advanced, is still that of a five, almost six-month-old, except in regards to the tongue and throat muscles that control speech, those are at the level of a one-year-old. It will remain to be seen if the mental development continues to outstrip the physical capabilities, or if those will catch up."

"She's brilliant. Like her mother." Nix said and smiled at Toya. She appeared relaxed. Far better than she had when the issue first presented itself.

"Indeed." Petra said dryly.

Overhead, NARA's measured tones announced that dinner would be ready in fifteen minutes. At the tail end of the announcement, an odd braying or bleating sounded. Selena shifted in her sleep, threatening to wake at any moment.

Petra's brow furrowed. "What the hell was that sound?"

"Bagpipes." Nix snickered. "Didn't you know it was Bagpipe Appreciation Day? At least, that's what Abdul said this morning."

"It's also National Crème brûlée Day." Toya added, trying hard not to laugh and failing miserably. "Which sounds delicious from how he described it."

Petra allowed a rare smile to spread over her face. "Bagpipes and crème brûlée for the win, I guess."

Selena, waking fully thanks to the announcement, parroted, "Creme brool-ay for win!"

Nix laughed at his daughter and lifted her out of her bassinet. "Indeed. Crème brûlée for the win."

The research would continue, but it was enough for one day's work. They walked out, the lights automatically dimming and extinguishing behind them as the braying of bagpipes played over the speakers.

The Earth Sees Me

06.08.2099
Ptolemy Lunar Base

Alone Bite sat alone, curled up inside of the ventilation shaft, reciting the book Annee read to her every night from memory.

"I see the earth and the earth sees me. Bless the earth and bless me. I see the sun and the sun sees me. Hello sun, how do you be?"

Bridget Kowalski, better known as Bite to the other colonists, was never supposed to have been born. A strict "no child" policy on the Ptolemy Lunar Colony was in everyone's best interests, after all. A baby carried in utero for the nine months it took would form in one-sixth the gravity of Earth, far too small an amount to recover from. It wouldn't just mean a life spent in a wheelchair, but one spent in agony, the heart struggling to pump, the lungs unable to fully inflate.

Until they could ensure that Ptolemy Lunar Colony could promise any future children a full life there on the Moon, without the still-necessary backup plan of evacuating to Earth, or even Mars, then it was a cruelty to bear a child in this frontier. And yet, here Bite was. Her tiny feet were constantly in motion, as she ran the lengths of the labyrinthine corridors deep beneath the Moon's surface and back to the viewing stations.

Her hair was cropped short, her clothing crudely sewn by her mother, adapted from the adult-sized jumpsuits. No matter that it had been five years since her rather surprising appearance, Annee Kowalski had yet to master the intricacies of hand sewing her daughter's garments.

No matter how hard she tried, Bite always looked like an underfed urchin. Her large green eyes and riot of red curls and pixie shaped nose made most of the adults around her smile. Her unbridled curiosity and constant questions less so, especially when coupled with a tendency towards taking functioning machines apart and occasionally losing their parts.

Bite would likely have argued that she hadn't actually *lost* the parts so much as she had *repurposed* them. She had learned, however, that adults didn't like it when she tried to explain. Either they became annoyed at her repurposing, or felt she was being argumentative. Annee had taught Bite to apologize and offer to fix the mistake.

As the only child growing up in the Ptolemy Lunar Colony, Bite was both bored and lonely. Despite this, Bridget "Bite" Kowalski was a brilliant young child. And that would have been apparent in minutes. Potty-trained at a year, thanks to the lack of proper diapers and significant maternal pressure, and speaking in full, concise sentences by age two, Bite was a handful in every sense of the word. At five years of age, mere months before the ESH outbreak wormed its way into their small colony, Bite was obsessed with creating a robot friend that would keep her company in the long hours of alone time.

The missing pieces of machines figured heavily into this, but that was a fact that the child kept to herself. Even her mother didn't know. Annee Kowalski had never intended to be a mother. She had shied away from the rather permanent option of having her uterus and ovaries removed. A common choice for those choosing a profession in low-g space. But she had bowed to her dying mother's request to delay it, potentially forever. And a month after her mother had died of leukemia, Annee had left Earth forever, her reproductive organs still intact, with a 99.99% guarantee from her OB/GYN that the birth control she received via a port the size of a computer chip would prevent any unwanted pregnancies.

"And 99.99% is not 100%." Annee was prone to say, after her surprise baby made a rather abrupt appearance on the Receiving Dock floor. It had been less than six months since Annee's lover died in a freak de-pressurization event. Julian had tried to shore up a collapsing tunnel deep below the lunar surface. She had been so lost to grief, and so sure of her birth control, she had not realized she was pregnant until she went into labor.

"You are nothing but a little bite of a child," the colony doctor had exclaimed, holding the tiny squalling infant. And with that comment, the nickname stuck.

"I see the earth and the earth sees me. Hello earth... will you dream with me?"

Until the virus. Until the death.

Now there was no one to call her anything. No one with a pulse, that is.

The smell had been the worst part of it. Far worse than the chaotic unfolding of the virus itself. For that, Bite had simply hidden. There were air vents far bigger than her throughout the lunar colony. Aside from a little dust, they had been perfect for curling up in. A few blankets and pillows, along with her VR headset, specially designed by Mick in Receiving to fit her smaller head, and her favorite vid collection, several bags of chips and Choco-Bites and she had whiled away the worst of it.

Annee had been one of the first to fall victim to it and afterward most of the adults close to Annee and Bite had also died. When Mick had fallen ill, he'd changed, and Bite had scurried into the air vents and hid from the others until finally, one day, the only noises to be heard were the machines.

The heaters.

The air.

The cleaner bots.

Not a single human voice left save her own.

Dead bodies smell terrible.

That was the lesson that Bite learned as she crept silently through the halls. She didn't know why she was alive, only that she was the only one. There might have been another, but she wasn't sure. The colony doctor. Bite had stepped into the infirmary and found the doctor, wrists cut open, blood congealed and black. By then, Bite had seen dozens of bodies, including her mother's. But finding the doctor, that had stuck in her dreams for a long time after. If Dr. Kenner had known Bite was alive, would she still have killed herself? Bite didn't think so. It was the loneliness that got to Dr. Kenner.

As Bite curled up in the air vents, her eyes slowly slipping closed, she felt as if she could understand how the doctor had felt. Being the only one left was lonely. Far lonelier than being the only child in the lunar colony.

Tales of Earth

Annee had regaled Bite with tales of growing up on Earth. From everything her mother said, it convinced Bite that Earth was a magical place for kids. Even the crowded high-rises of the super-cities where stepping outside was a rare event. Annee had grown up in a giant skyscraper, one that occupied an entire city block and had everything they needed inside of it, even schools.

"I rarely went anywhere else," she said. "I remember how odd it felt to be out on street level and look up and see the enormous sky above, full of clouds and flitters. And on the rarest of days? Sunlight!"

"What did it feel like, Annee?" Bite had tried on Mom, Mama, even Mommy, but nothing had ever felt quite right. Her mother preferred her to call her Annee, and so she did. "The sun, that is?"

Her mother had laughed. "I've told you this before."

"I like to hear it. Tell me again. Please?"

Annee had sighed, sat back, pulled Bite up against her. "The sun is warm on Earth. It's warm here too, but the atmosphere is too thin."

"Tell me about the beach again."

Her mother had rolled her eyes.

"Please!"

"Fine, fine." She had run a hand along Bite's arm, fiddled with one ragged cuff of her poorly hemmed jumpsuit. "It was a warm day, and we piled onto a large transport. Everyone in my class got to go. All four hundred and thirty-two of us. It was a long trip. Longer than traveling on the surface or even underneath on the old subways. We had to leave early in the morning. The transport took us all the way to this old boardwalk. Years ago it had been an amusement park, before virtual reality really took off and everyone stopped going to the parks."

She had paused then, and Bite sensed her mother was trying to get out of telling the story. She noticed this a lot with her mom and wondered if her mom missed Earth. Bite found the stories of a sun so big and so far away that still made things warm for Earth, but not for the Moon, incredible and confusing. She didn't understand the atmosphere yet, not enough for it to seem anything more than whimsical and almost magical. And water, water so deep that it covered your entire body, and could be hundreds if not thousands of meters deep, sounded impossible, and yet Annee swore it was true.

"Don't stop," Bite had begged.

Annee had sighed, then described the corpse of a rollercoaster, rusted and creaky, no longer in use. The buildings housed antique pinball and video games. They sold cotton candy. Just five Ameros for a ball of whipped sugar the size of your head. This led to the part where Annee had gotten a sunburn because her teacher had forgotten the sunscreen and the ozone layer was so thin that twenty minutes on a hazy day would make you pay for a week after.

"Do you miss it?" Bite had asked, suddenly far more curious about that than about hearing how the sun could give you a sunburn, which sounded painful and rather deadly, although her mother was obviously alive so it couldn't have killed her.

"What? The ocean?"

"No. Earth. Do you miss it?"

Her mother had turned away, picked at some invisible piece of lint and sighed. "There's no actual point in missing something you will never see again."

Annee had said this more than once and Bite couldn't help wondering if that was true true, or just sort of true. Lots of things the adults said were sort of true, but not the real true true. She had known this, even then, before everyone died. There were things adults didn't say, truths they thought were too big for a little kid like her. Bite didn't think they were right, but that didn't really matter. In the end, they had all taken their sort of truths, and true truths, and they had died. Even Annee. They had died and Bite remained here, alone.

Before Annee had died though, she had told Bite all the stories, good and bad, sort of true, but more often than not, the true true ones. It was enough to fill Bite's mind in the long, lonely moments after.

Somehow Some Way

Bodies smell. Not just that, but they get gross. That was what Bite had learned in the intervening days and weeks and months. First, a dead person looked just like they were sleeping. Well, at least in most cases. Some had coughed up blood or died violently, and those were just yucky from the get go. But most of the others died, and unless their eyes were open, they looked like they had just fallen down and gone to sleep. At least, that's how they looked at first. Then, they turned gray, or worse, purple and black on the face if they went down face first. Then they swelled up and stunk. This sickly sweet, foul smell that filled the air, even creeping into the air vents where Bite slept and making everything smell bad, even her clothes and food. After stinking for a while, this black stuff slipped out of them. Their skin cracked and split from the swelling, and the blackness seeped out. Maybe it was blood, or guts, Bite wasn't sure, but it was nasty. As if all a person was - their personality, their likes and dislikes, the jokes, even the grumpiness, all dissolved into blackness. Bite had nightmares that the bodies would dissolve into rivers of black goo and get all over everything, and then *she* would turn into black goo because it had to be contagious, just like the ESH virus had been.

Little scientist that she was, Bite realized quickly that not all bodies acted the same. The black goo came out of some depending upon the "ambient conditions." And when she asked NARA, she learned it was called putrescine and, combined with hydrogen sulphide, methane, and cadaverine, were the by-products of decomposition. But other bodies, depending on their location, reacted differently. The ones in Receiving, for example, with its high ceilings and frigid, dry air, the skin turned leathery, and they didn't swell so much as they seemed to dry up. She noticed this as she scurried past Mick and the others who had fallen in various locations throughout the cavernous space. Bite hated seeing the bodies. She missed them, even Allen Radinger, who would glare at her and complain to Bite's mother that she was "underfoot yet again." Bite hated leaving her little hideaway in the air vents, but she needed to do something about the bodies, and that would take access to the Robotics Lab, and to do that, she had to go through Receiving.

Once past the bodies, and thanks to the chillier nature of Receiving, the smell receded significantly. Bite had been a regular in Robotics for the past six months or more. Prior to the outbreak, she'd gotten in trouble with Annee regularly by sneaking off there. Mick had taken her under his wing, and showed her how to solder, to assemble the various components, and he had taught Bite how to code. Simple things at first, and then lines of code that had grown progressively more difficult.

"Here, read this," he'd said, and his fingers had danced briefly on his tablet along with a whoosh before chiming on her tablet as an incoming message. "That's your homework. Learn that, and you can get the bots to make their own bots."

A week later, he was dead. One of the last to be infected by the virus. Before he'd lost his mind to it, he'd made sure Bite had everything she needed. Whether it was access to the food stores or any part of the colony previously beyond her reach. It was Mick who had told her to hide, even as the virus affected his reasoning. He'd looked at her with such a hungry, desperate expression that it turned the gentle giant she had known all of her brief life into something rather frightening, something to be afraid of. After that, he'd sent her regular notifications on her tablet. Most of them were granting access and sharing passcodes to the various parts of the lunar colony that a five-year-old child had no place going under normal circumstances. But nothing about the ESH virus, or Bite's very existence, was normal.

He'd left a brief note as well. "You'll need to get rid of the bodies, kid. Somehow, some way, but it needs doing. Repurpose some bots to get it done."

She had yet to go to most of the "no go" sections of the colony. No need, really. She visited an empty guest suite to take her weekly shower and use the facilities. It was just halfway down the corridor from her nest in the air vents. And she had learned not to gorge on the massive container of Choco-Snax in the Food Storage. Doing so had given her the runs, and she only had a handful of outfits. Cleaning poop off of them had not been a pleasant experience. Eventually, she might design a bot to wash clothes, something she was quite keen on since it was not a job she liked to do, but for now, she had washed them off and let them drip dry.

The major systems on the lunar colony ran without need for human interference, leaving Bite to wander about the place with hours upon hours of a day to fill with some kind of activity and more food than she could consume in ten years sitting in Food Storage. Those hours ended up being filled with coding the bots. She needed several of them, after all.

The bodies, the smell of them, and, to be honest, their simple *presence* was too much. Bite could barely eat, the smell was so bad. And just the sight of them, scattered as they were throughout the corridors, and in their billets, and well, everywhere. She picked at her food, nauseated most days. The bots she was currently coding would build the next generation, at least two, possibly three, larger bots that could move large weights. She needed them to be versatile enough to grab, lift, and lever each body from wherever it lay to the large bay in Receiving where the massive airlocks sat. Two sets of doors. The first opened into a room large enough to contain one of the moonbus rovers with ease. And the bots would need to retrieve each body, take it to the airlock, and then, once inside, the inner doors would close and the outer would open. They then would need to take the bodies outside, to join the others already piled there.

The sooner she could get this done, the better. The bodies mushy with the black putrescine continued to turn to goo, and the stink was awful. Bite suspected it would be worse before it got better. After all, there were at least fifty bodies inside of their individual quarters. Once she ordered the bots to open those doors, the smells would circulate even more. She'd brought an MRE of maple and spice oatmeal with her. Another MRE, chicken cacciatore, for later. Just looking at the MREs caused her tiny stomach to roil and Bite turned away, any hunger she had already slipped away. Better to work on the last of the coding.

Six Months

It had taken a while, longer than she had imagined, to take care of most of the bodies. Some were impossible. Their positioning inside of their rooms, several bodies had fallen in front of the door, blocking the door from opening at all, or state of decay, had made it impossible to get them all. The bots had done what they could, but some actions were beyond even them. Any of those bodies were behind doors she did not need to access, and Bite shrugged it off. The smell was gone, finally, and her appetite had returned.

The only thing she wanted for was company, and that was an ache she could not seem to will away. Bite talked to NARA more and more. But NARA wasn't enough. Bite ached to hear other voices, familiar voices, but they were all dead. And one morning, still blinking the sleep out of her eyes, she had an idea.

"NARA, access all voice recordings of Annee Kowalski."

"Accessing."

"Compile and use this voice for all communications prefaced with the word Annee." Even now she could not think of her mother as Mom or Mommy. Annee was her mother, sure, but always it was Annee, even now.

"Done." NARA responded.

"Annee," Bite said, "tell me a story."

Annee's voice came through the speaker. "What story would you like to hear?"

It was her mother's voice, but not at the same time. Bite felt a wave of misery wash over her. It wasn't the same. It would never be the same. She was alone. There was no one left to love her, to care, and perhaps there wasn't anyone left on Earth either. Perhaps she was the only one in the whole of humanity. And even if she wasn't, would anyone think to come and find her?

"What story would you like to hear?" Annee's voice repeated, but Bite knew it wasn't her mother. It was just a sound bite, a reproduction. That's all it could be.

"Never mind." Bite said and thought hard about what to do. She would be six years old soon. The lunar colony had sat in silence for just over six months, and for all that Earth knew, there were no survivors on the Ptolemy Lunar Base. "NARA, play all recordings of Annee Kowalski's voice since her arrival on base on all devices."

"Playing all recordings of Kowalski, Annee since arrival on base on 14 April 2092." NARA responded.

Bite let the recordings play day and night. It was reassuring, in a way. The silence before it had been overwhelming. Nothing but the machines pumping, the air circulating, to keep her company. The moon was a silent place. No traffic, or birds, or background noises. Bite had watched enough of the vids from Earth to know that sound was everywhere on Earth. Even in a field, birds, hundreds of them, could make noise. The recordings didn't weed out ambient noise in the background or other people's voices. A year into the recordings, Bite finally heard her father's voice for the first time as Annee greeted him in the cafeteria, welcoming him to the lunar colony. Flirting with each other.

Bite didn't understand it all. The flirting, or what she would later come to understand, was flirting, confused her. So did the sounds of her mother as she cried out in the bed she had eventually shared with Julian. Bite ended up asking NARA to fast forward anytime her mother sounded as if she were in pain. Doing so, however, meant she missed her father's sudden death, and her own birth a few months later, another year into the recordings. And once the recordings had ended, she had asked NARA to play them again, and again, and again.

There was something comforting about it. More so than the recordings of anyone else in the colony, even her father's, who she had never met. Although, from what Bite could tell, he had been nice, kind, just as her mother had described him the few times Bite could get her to speak of him.

Later, when she could repeat nearly every conversation word for word, she asked NARA for other voices. Mick's in particular, especially when she struggled over a line of code or felt stuck. The Robotics lab was the room she spent the most time in. She moved her bedding into a corner of the lab and created a nest out of blankets and pillows. The steady hum of the machines lulled her to sleep and woke her gently each morning.

A Touch of Art

Time unspooled itself slowly. Despite there being no one there to tell her when to sleep or when to wake, Bite took it upon herself to create reminders. NARA would chime an alert each evening, announcing in Annee's voice, "Time to brush your teeth, Bite." The sonic toothbrush and toothpaste pellets waited in a nearby empty billet. Once weekly, her mother's voice would remind her to shower, and three times a day, a gentle chime would remind her it was time for a meal.

The Ptolemy Lunar Colony was well-built, and the systems chugged on. Even the hydroponics section was self-sufficient to a degree, and Bite only really cared for the strawberries, anyway. The micro-greens had never appealed. They grew full, overflowed their containers, and eventually died away.

She had finally moved out of the ventilation shaft and into a spare room, one that hadn't been assigned to any of the former inhabitants. She had left it undecorated for the longest time, months, before realizing that in this empty place, she could please herself. Bite found an ebook in the online files that showed beautiful pictures of the Earth's greatest wonders. She couldn't help but imagine how they would look on the long, boring walls of the hallways she walked each day. The numbers of electrical components available to her now kept her busy as well. Slowly, Bite made her way through a wealth of lessons that Mick had prepared for her before he died. She took what she learned and created bots that could recreate the scenic images of Earth, as well as keep her company in the long, lonely days.

Bite resolved to learn to dance one day after watching a vintage Bollywood movie, entranced by the gyrating figures on the screen. And that led to ballroom dance, rumba, ballet, and even yoga.

One afternoon, when listening to some of NARAs recordings of two visiting Chinese scientists, who had visited on a cooperative mission when she was just a baby, they inspired her to learn Mandarin. Eventually, her language 'bot taught her German, French, and Latin as well.

Bite lost track of the number of books she read. She tore through the scores of children's books and discovered a cache of science fiction that fascinated her. It was dated, written well over a century ago, and amusingly inaccurate, but she enjoyed many of the author's books. Podkayne of Mars, especially. She wished she could go to Mars and spent several weeks immersing herself in everything she could find about the planet, fact and fiction.

Occasionally, Bite would stop, go to the broad viewing port at the mouth of the lava tube and gaze out at the Earth, hanging full and heavy in the sky. She tried to imagine how it really felt there. Was the sun really warm on your face? Warm enough for a sunburn? And the gravity, did it hurt? She would stare at the deep blue seas, the continents clothed in green and grown, and wonder at the white cloud cover, ever-fluctuating and moving. Once, she had seen what could only have been a hurricane, so slow it didn't appear to be moving, creep up the side of a continent over a period of days.

The years slid by.

Arrival

The sound of the massive airlock doors in Receiving opening had been a shock. So much so that it sent Bite scurrying for the ventilation shafts. It had been years, and she had grown. It wasn't as easy as it once had been to climb in and hide. Her bolt hole was dustier than she remembered and far more cramped.

She could barely breathe. Was it aliens? Her mind ran wild. Perhaps aliens had seeded Earth with the ESH virus in order to claim it for their own. Perhaps the Moon was a stop along the way to their massive ships setting up orbit in Earth's skies.

The voices, however, chased the fear of aliens away and exchanged it for another, nameless, wordless fear. Others. People she didn't know. What would they think of her? Would they be angry with how she had changed things? The murals? The bots?

"I'm telling you, Setara, I saw something on the cameras. More a *someone*, only small, like a midget." The voice wasn't far away. A man's. Not low and growly like Mick's had been, but definitely different from the gentle one that laughed in return.

"A *midget*, Rick? Seriously?"

"Well, how the hell do you explain it? It's not like there are any kids here on the Moon, other than Arie and the multitudes in Cryo. I wouldn't have seen it if I hadn't been looking for the main broadcast switch to turn off the voices." The voices were closer now. "Christ, these murals. I've seen nothing like it. Have you?"

The dust inside of the ventilation shaft tickled Bite's nose, and she screwed up her face, her nose itching like mad. She didn't think they sounded dangerous. The man's voice seemed like he was in awe of the artwork, not angry. Should she emerge from her hiding place?

"That there is the Golden Gate Bridge. I saw the remains of it once. Just the foundation remained after the Big One hit back in '69. It's a visitor's center now." The soft-spoken voice the man had called Setara said in return. She sounded nice. Kind. Bite wondered if she was pretty. Annee had been pretty, but sad, as if she lived in a world of perpetual loss and disappointment.

Bite's eyes watered, and the need to sneeze was rising to an intolerable level. She wished they would keep walking. For all that she had hoped and dreamed over the years that someone, anyone, would come to the lunar base and she wouldn't be alone, that reality was suddenly quite overwhelming.

Every single day for the past four years, Bite had heard the voices of the dead over the speakers. Not just that, she'd learned their secrets. She had learned that Dr. Kenner had lost her three daughters, first to divorce and then to the ESH virus. That Mick had learned he had an inoperable brain tumor just two weeks before the virus ravaged the Ptolemy Lunar Colony. She had listened to the doctor discussing with Annee the reality that Bite had always known, that the only home she would ever know was the Moon. Born and bred in low-g gravity, her bones hadn't formed well enough to adapt to Earth gravity. She realized then why her mother had been sad. Bite's birth was a life sentence. She could never leave this place, never climb a mountain or breathe fresh air. It bothered her far less than it must have Annee. It is harder to miss what you have never had.

"There's someone still here, Rick." Setara's voice lowered, and Bite struggled to hear what she said next because the dust and her nose were at an impasse and in that moment, Bite sneezed.

The sneeze was an explosion of sound amplified by the air vent she was currently hiding in. It rolled and rattled and seconds later, after a second and third convulsion of violent sneezing rolled through her, a dark-skinned face was peering up and in at her. Framed in dark curls, the woman smiled at her. She had the whitest teeth Bite had ever seen, with a slight gap between the top two. Bite blinked back at her.

"Is it the midget?" Rick's voice behind her, out of sight, asked.

Setara rolled her eyes and smiled wider. "No, it's not a midget, Rick. Hand me that stool there, please. Go on ahead and give us a minute, will you?"

"Seriously, Set?" Rick asked, and when the woman didn't respond, Bite could hear his steps retreat. "All right, but if it bites or has rabies, you're on your own."

Setara rolled her eyes again and shook her head. Bite was trying to find the words to say hello, but the words wouldn't come. This wasn't a 'bot that required concise instructions. It wasn't one of her teacher bots that expected a correct answer, properly enunciated, in Latin or Mandarin. This was flesh and blood, here in front of her, smiling in a way that reminded Bite of a darker-skinned, happier version of her mother.

The woman waited until Rick's footsteps receded down the hall. "He's harmless. Just a big joker, really. Nothing to worry about."

"I'm not scared." Bite answered, her voice cracking. She felt like crying and she did not know why. After wishing and wishing for someone, anyone, to come, now she was ready for them to leave.

"Okay." Setara said in response. "You know, I have a daughter. She's ten. Her name is Arie."

Bite chewed on this for a minute. The impending tears backed off. She was nearly ten now, too. Was this woman trying to trick her? Tell her what she wanted to hear? Convince her to come out and then... what?

Setara pulled back out of the entrance and Bite heard the stool move, shift. The woman sighed. "This mural is amazing. All of them, everywhere. Did you do them?"

"No. The bots did. I told them what I wanted, though." Bite answered and shifted her own body. The shaft was so much smaller now than it had been when she was little. She knew she had been growing, because her jumpsuits didn't fit well anymore. Bite had slowly unrolled the arm and leg cuffs until the bottom of the pants legs were nearly to her knees and the sleeves fell short of her elbows. She wished Setara was still peering in, but also she felt a little relieved she wasn't because it was scary being that close to another human being.

"Well, they are amazing. I want to see every single one. I think this is something that really makes the place special." She was silent for a moment, and Bite held her breath, not sure what would come next. "I heard a story once." Setara said, still out of sight. "About a little girl on the moon. A real little girl, growing up surrounded by adults, with no other children to play with. Her name was Beatrice, no, no, Bridget. Is your name Bridget?"

"Bite."

"Hm?" Setara asked, leaning back in. Bite nearly scuttled backwards, but Setara wasn't reaching or grasping, and so Bite stopped, held her ground.

"They called me Bite. Because I was so small."

Setara smiled and Bite couldn't help but feel as if it was the most beautiful thing she had seen in a long time. The tears gathered again.

"Well, Bite, I think you've grown a bit since then, but you still are just a bite of a thing. So the name definitely fits! I think Arie has at least three centimeters on you. If you come out, I could measure you properly and see."

Moments later, Bite gathered every bit of courage she could find and climbed out of the ventilation shaft. She was dusty, and her skin had taken on a gray tinge of the lunar dust. She stared up at the first person she had seen in four years.

Setara was taller than Bite, but she seemed to remember adults being even taller than that. Or had she truly grown that much? The woman moved slowly, giving Bite plenty of room.

"I don't bite. It's just a name." Bite said, brushing at the dust, suddenly painfully aware of how she must look. Her cut down threadbare jumpsuit was snagged and torn, permanently soiled with food and machine grease. Bite couldn't remember the last time she had washed it and the material was stiff now. No amount of washing seemed to fix that. She had given up on her hair. When it grew into her eyes, she cut it. The tangles and snarls condensed into a bird's nest of of matted hair. Bite was acutely aware of it now as she stared at Setara's neatly braided hair. Bite wondered if she smelled. Setara wasn't wrinkling up her nose or anything, but Bite was pretty sure she could smell herself. She'd been so busy with the latest set of bots that she'd forgotten to wash.

Setara laughed. "I figured as much. Don't mind Rick, he thinks he's quite the comedian. My goodness, you are taller than you looked, all scrunched up in there." She bit her lip, a small frown on her face. "You've been here all along. With no one?"

Damn the tears. Bite struggled to see Setara. Her eyes welling up. Inside, it felt like a war was being fought. She wanted to run away, even from this kind, smiling woman and hide, hide, hide. The fear practically gibbered at her. People. *People.* People she didn't know. They hadn't known she was here. Hadn't expected her. What if they didn't want her? What if...

"Oh, Bite. Sweetheart." Setara's voice softened, and Bite's tears fell, gushing out, a torrent of sadness and fear and loneliness that Bite hadn't realized was waiting there. "Can I..." Setara's warm hands reached out to touch Bite, undid the last vestige of control she had. She fell into the woman's arms, sobbing, choking. She hadn't cried like this when Mick died, not even when she lost her mother, Annee. It was as if every moment of loss and loneliness had led to this moment. Bite felt as if she was dissolving. As if she hadn't really existed. If no one knew of you, did you even really exist?

Setara's arms enveloped her, pulling her close, as close as Annee would. Bite could feel the woman's lips press into her rank, hopelessly tangled hair, her breath warm and comforting. Bite cried harder. Her entire body shook.

"It's okay, Bite. It's okay to be sad and scared. And I promise you, Bite, I promise you, I will make sure you are never, ever alone again." She held Bite, crooned to her as one would a tiny baby, holding her close, rocking her. Bite sobbed and shook until her head felt stuffed with cotton and achy, and her body felt heavy, and so, so tired. Slowly, the tears stopped and, even slower, the shaking, until she realized she was sitting in Setara's lap like a small child would. A flash of embarrassment must have shown on her face, because Setara hugged her again and said, "Never ever be self-conscious about showing emotion, Bite. It is what makes us human. And we have all lost far too much to hold those emotions in."

Bite nodded, wondering for a moment who Setara had lost as Setara released her gently. She stood up and realized they were no longer alone. There were more of them. Far more than just the man called Rick and Setara. Her eyes widened as Bite seriously considered returning to her bolt hole. There were at least ten people in the hallway, varying expressions of disbelief, shock, and what might have been sympathy on their faces. They didn't look angry or mad, though, and Bite wondered if maybe, just maybe, she would be okay. It was hard to breathe, though, with so many people there.

Setara stood, her graceful limbs unfolding. She set a hand on Bite's shoulder and addressed the others.

"This is Bite. She has been caring for the lunar station and waiting for us to arrive. I'm sure she will answer all of our questions in time. For now, though, I think she needs some privacy and time to get used to us."

The crowd of people slowly dispersed, a buzz of murmured conversations leaving with them. Bite gulped. She felt drained and her head was pounding. Still, Bite could feel a smile forming on her lips. She wasn't alone. For the first time in a very long time, she wasn't alone.

She Dreams of Earth

"Bite? Can you come in here for a moment?" Setara called out to Bite. She was curled up with a book waiting for Arie to finish her homework. Bite had already finished hers, but her friend hadn't, and looked up from her equations with a mournful expression.

Setara had insisted that Arie was revived from Cryo in the days following the lifeship's arrival on the surface of the Moon. "At least for a little while, Bite, you can have what most children on Earth have, a friend to get up to mischief with." She had winked at Bite when she said this, which was how Bite knew Setara was teasing her. Sometimes, after all these years alone, even with the vids, Bite took things too literally. Thankfully, Setara seemed to sense this and helped explain such things.

Bite unfolded herself from the bunk below Arie's and walked into the common room outside of her and Arie's bedroom. There were two other adults sitting with Setara, a woman she had seen on the first day, the other, a gaunt, dark-haired man, who was unfamiliar to her. They looked at her and Bite felt a quiver of fear run through her. What did they want?

The past three weeks with Setara and Arie had been nothing short of magical. Especially Arie, who was funny and kind, like her mother. Arie looked like a miniature Setara, right down to the bright white smile and braided hair. They had settled in together, with only a few hiccups, and Bite had shown Arie every inch of the colony. Well, not every inch. The team had moved in and the wide access Bite had enjoyed was now curtailed slightly. Which was fine, really. She had no need of most of the areas, although she missed waltzing into the Food Storage area anytime she felt like it. And at first, the older man working in Robotics was taken aback by her presence there one morning when he arrived for his shift. It had taken some getting used to. Apparently, children on Earth were kept in school for years and years and kept out of places of work, except on special occasions. Bite didn't really understand it, and thought it silly, but she adapted. Besides, spending her days with Arie was better than learning ballroom dancing from her favorite 'bot Georgia, or conjugating French verbs with Ferdinand. The bots didn't have the emotion, the delight, or bright-eyed interest that Arie had. And if all that weren't enough, the second day Bite had spent showing Arie all the secret places, nooks and crannies hidden about the colony, Arie had told her they were "official besties" and well, Bite had never had one of those.

"Bite, sweetheart, this is Kim Westover and Brian Leeds. Brian came down from the Sana this morning to meet you." Setara said, pointing to each. "Will you come sit with us? Brian has a question for you."

Bite came in and sat down next to Setara. The older woman put her arm around her, running her long, tapered fingers through Bite's newly shorn hair. It was short, shorter than Bite ever remembered it being, but necessary. The hair had been too tangled to save. Since then, however, Setara had shown her how to care for it. Each evening, she would gently brush Bite's hair, just as she would style Arie's in the morning. Bite leaned into Setara, seeking the woman's warmth and reassurance. Even now, after weeks of the lunar team in place and the corridors once again filled with people, being around others was often difficult for her. She was comfortable with Setara and Arie, but the others, not as much.

Brian leaned forward and smiled at her. "I've heard so much about you, Bite. And I've seen the bots you created throughout the colony. The artwork and murals make this place very special."

Bite gave a small smile back. "They are of places on Earth."

He grinned then. "Yes. I've visited a few of them. Do you ever think of visiting Earth, Bite?"

Bite shook her head. "Can't."

"Because you were born here."

She nodded. "Annee, my mom, she said that a baby's bones don't form right in low-g. My bones aren't strong enough. I wouldn't be able to breathe. My muscles aren't strong enough either."

Brian nodded. "Your mom was right. At least she was. Recently, things have changed. There have been some new therapies recently, and I've been on a team that is studying those recent developments. I understand you know something about coding and electronics. Is that correct?"

"Mick taught me." Bite said, and Brian's face changed.

"You knew Mick Santiago?"

Bite hadn't known his last name, but she nodded all the same.

"He was a friend. A colleague. We roomed together in college half a lifetime ago." He looked sad.

"He was my friend, too." Bite looked down at her hands, twisted them in her lap. She didn't like to remember the last few hours of Mick's life. When the virus had taken hold and he had lost most of who he was. He'd shouted at her, told her to run and hide. She had. As fast as her legs could carry her. And when she had come out, everyone, including Mick, was dead.

Brian cleared his throat. "All over the world, and beyond, scientists have been working on a cure for ESH, but also for other things. There is this new technology that I've been studying, one that could help our bodies recover from ESH, so that women can have children again, but also it can repair brain cells, muscles, even bone. It could repair *you*, Bite." He said. "It's experimental, but there are multiple examples of it working and repairing not just our ability to have children again, but even repairing brain damage, organ failure, and re-growing lost limbs. Setara told me about you, and I, well, we, think that if you had these nanites injected into you, they could repair your body enough that you could return to Earth with us."

"Return?" Bite looked up at Setara, fear coursing through her. Were they leaving? "You aren't... staying?"

Setara pulled her close. "We aren't going anywhere for a long time, Bite. The asteroid hasn't even reached Earth yet, and it will be at least nine years after Impact, possibly longer, before Earth recovers. That's a long time from now, but yes, eventually we must return to Earth."

Bite felt as if they had plunged a knife into her stomach. Sick dread formed at the thought of Arie and Setara leaving.

"But you promised..."

"And I'm keeping that promise, Bite. This is the way to keep it. The nanites can help you. They *will* help you. And you will return to Earth with us. You would have a life there."

The woman, Kim, spoke then. "Bite, they have assigned me to be your advocate since your mother is gone." She looked at Setara. "Mrs. Lafayette, erm, Setara, has asked to become your custodial parent and, I am inclined to grant it since it seems you are settling in well, but because of your circumstances, you are still a ward of the Terran United Planetary Government, and I must give permission for this experimental therapy."

Bite looked from Setara back to Kim. "Okay."

Kim frowned slightly. "Bite, there are no guarantees, and should you undertake the treatment, they will place you in a medically induced coma for an as yet undetermined period because of the still experimental nature of the nanite therapy."

Bite blinked at this, confused.

"It might be painful, Bite." Setara said, her hand on Bite's shoulder. "Which is why you would be unconscious during the therapy. So you wouldn't be in pain or suffer needlessly."

"I'll be asleep." Bite stated.

"Yes." Both women answered.

"Will I dream?"

Brian smiled at that. "Most patients report they do not dream."

"And when I wake up, I'll be better? Able to go to Earth?"

"That's the plan. But I need to tell you we don't know for sure. Maybe your body can only be prepared for a lower-gravity environment, such as Mars. They are…"

"Thirty-eight percent of Earth, just over twice that of the Moon." Bite finished his sentence. Brian beamed at her.

"Yes, exactly." He leaned forward, pressing his hands together as if in prayer, "We shoot for the goal of Earth gravity, but if we can't get that, if it exceeds the nanites' capabilities, then we can surely reach Mars-level capacity. And the settlement on Mars has sped up the terraforming. A stint in Cryo and you would wake up to a world with breathable air and gravity that you could exist and thrive in."

Bite glanced back at Setara, who nodded reassuringly. "It's a chance at a life outside of domes, a chance to breathe fresh air, Bite."

Bite thought of the stories her mother had told her of Earth. Mountains that were so big, you couldn't climb to the top of them in a day. Oceans filled with thousands of meters of water. Buildings out in the open. An atmosphere. A place where water could fall from the sky. Wind. Dirt. They were all such alien things. Impossibilities. Legend.

"Okay."

It took three separate treatments of nanites over the next eight years. At each major growth spurt, back under, she would go. Arie, because she was still growing, underwent the standard muscle and bone stimulation regime that had, until then, been given only to adults. It allowed the girls to grow up, side by side, together.

Arie and Bite did everything together. Even during the transformative and angst-ridden teen years, their bond grew. Best friends, as close, if not more so, than sisters, and Setara served as mother to them both.

Bite learned that Arie and Setara had lost as well. Lee, Setara's husband and Arie's father, had fallen to the ESH virus, as had Setara's unborn child. For the legion of others that moved through the corridors of the Ptolemy Lunar Colony, Bite remained withdrawn. The years alone had taken their toll and being around others remained difficult. With Setara and Arie, she was happy, even carefree and bubbly. The murals, which Bite had instructed the bots to create, covered every inch of the colony walls, even the private spaces that she had not entered or had access to. They put the bots to work on those spaces as well, finishing what Bite had started.

After the first treatment, which lasted six months, Bite emerged from her coma three inches taller and two shoe sizes larger. A host of images of the newly finished work of the bots also greeted her in the various billets. She was a bit of a celebrity there on the Moon. The little girl who lived all alone on the Moon for four years.

Brian, a familiar face by now, sat across from her. He grinned, and she knew that meant he had good news for her. "Bite, I have great news."

"Actually, I prefer to be called Bridget now."

He blinked and nodded. "Of course. *Bridget*. I have fantastic news. Your bone density is right where we want it, as are the other muscles, including your heart. I've shared all of your reports with Leonard Snelling on Mars and with several colleagues better versed in the muscular-skeletal changes that were needed for you to be comfortable in Earth gravity and they are all in agreement."

He practically sang the last sentence, "The nanites have successfully remediated your body and I see no reason you cannot return to Earth with the lifeships in sixteen months."

Setara, sitting on the left side of her, and Arie on the right, both squeezed her hands. Earth. She was going to go to Earth. An impossible dream until eight years ago, and merely a hope and a prayer until now. Bridget let out a breath, as her chest relaxed, loosened. She wouldn't be left behind when the lifeships returned to Earth. Bridget would go with them. She wasn't alone and never had to be, never again.

Brian left shortly after. She couldn't remember if she had thanked him, or really what she had said in response to the news. Even during the treatments, she hadn't wanted to hope, couldn't allow herself that. But now, after years of poking and prodding, of machines, needles, and tiny machines swimming through her. Two near misses, once when her heart stopped in an aberrant moment and they brought her back, all while she was comatose, and here was the reward. The promise delivered on.

The only thing that Brian had been wrong about?

While in the medically induced comas, she *had* dreamed. She dreamed of Earth.

The Kiss of the Ocean

Bridget sat in the flitter and stared at the vastness of it. How often had she seen it in the old vids? Too often to count. And yet, here she was, humbled by the sheer enormity of it. Being outside still felt awkward. Two decades of walls, ceilings, where the biggest thing she knew was the Receiving Bay. Well, that was until the Vision lifeship landed and the Sana established orbit around the Moon. The trips on the shuttle and lander back and forth between the two lifeships had been a grand adventure, although seeing that many people all in one place, sleeping in Cryo or not, had planted in her a wish to run back to the ventilation shafts and hide as she had done when the first team had arrived.

The sky above was endless. The fluffy white wisps of clouds scudded across the sky, whipped by a wind from the west. North, south, east, and west. These meant something now. More than just a corridor branching off in one direction or the other. The air smelled different too, unusual. The roar of the waves as they crashed against the shoreline was louder than Bridget had imagined it would be.

She had done her research. The beach that Annee had described, the one she had visited as a child growing up, was the same one. Altered, obviously. The ocean had risen hundreds of feet after Impact. It had bulldozed everything in sight, annihilating it as if they had made it of paper.

There were a few twisted lumps of steel where the rollercoaster might have been, a scattering of artifacts that others far more familiar with the coastline would likely recognize as belonging to a structure. Bridget knew it only from Annee's stories and old vids. Ten years had passed since Impact, and over fifteen more than that since her mother had seen it in person. Unlike the Moon, where everything stayed the same, the Earth seemed to do nothing *but* change. The ocean etched the shoreline, ever changing it, through shifting sands and tides. Trees grew, and forests fell. The world was old, far older than anything Bridget had seen in the tiny lunar colony that had been her entire existence until now.

The communicator in her breast pocket chirped. "Bridget? Did you find the beach?" Arie's voice sounded in the earbud in her left ear. Bridget grinned, even though Arie couldn't see her.

"Yeah, I sure did."

"How is it?"

"Really, really big."

Arie giggled. "That's what you say about everything. How's the water?"

"I don't know yet."

"Wait, what?" was Arie's befuddled response. "Your locater says you've been stationary for the past fifteen minutes."

"I just..." Bridget's voice caught. Some part of her had dreamed of seeing Annee here. A ghost of her, even a flash of light or her face in clouds, something. "I uh, I'm still in the flitter."

"Bridget..." Arie's voice softened, "Bite. I should have come with you."

"I'm okay, really, I am. In fact, I'm getting out now."

"I could requisition one and be there in twenty minutes." Arie said, sounding concerned. "They can spare me for a few hours."

"You don't have to do that, Arie."

"Yeah, I think I do. I don't know what I was thinking of taking a shift on your birthday. You deserve better than that. I'll see you in twenty. What are besties for, after all?"

A low tone sounded, showing Arie had disconnected, and Bridget felt a surge of happiness. She hadn't wanted to ask, not with everyone so busy, but somehow, Arie had understood.

She climbed out of the flitter and stepped onto the sun-warmed sand, surprised at how her feet sunk into it. Grains of it slipped into her shoes and she leaned against the door of the flitter and slipped them both off, leaving them behind. The ocean was less than two hundred feet away. The smell of it, a briny, fishy smell, was slowly growing on her. Earth seemed filled with unusual smells. Mostly wonderful. The air smelled sweeter and fresher than anything she had ever smelled before. Bridget couldn't help wondering if the others knew how magical and beautiful this world was.

There was a fair-sized creek cutting through the sand and feeding directly into the ocean. The water in it was ice cold. No surprise there, it was being fed by the small glacier that rose in the distance. The team assigned to monitor the Earth had delayed the lifeships' return for a year because of the mini-ice age that Impact had engendered. The glaciers were nowhere near the size of those from the tail end of the last century. They existed, however, and were quickly diminishing with the return of the sun and the warming trend Earth was once again experiencing. Soon the glaciers would be gone.

The roar of the ocean was louder than ever. The force of the waves crashing caused a steady breeze to buffet Bridget's hair, now approaching shoulder-length since she no longer had to keep it short due to water restrictions. She wanted to explore the ocean, learn how the creatures within it had fared after Impact. Her mind strayed, notes on what kind of submersible was needed, and how she could automate it. Since landing, they received word of all kinds of survivors, including some in the Mediterranean Sea, where an ocean spiral city had survived Impact. She had learned of people hiding in caves, mountains, and more - eking out survival in the tiny pockets and corners of the world. How they did it, how they survived, made her four lonely years alone on the Moon seem trivial and small.

The sand underfoot had turned from warm, and almost silky smooth on the skin of her feet to cold, thick, and caked. She walked closer. The water rushed in then, cold, almost as cold as the water from the glacier, foam surging around her ankles, sand disappearing from under her feet. The ocean pulled at her to come closer. A siren song of danger, to be sure. Of all the long and rather impressive list of things she had learned, alone in the lunar base for four years, or with the others in the decade that followed, learning how to swim was not on that list. Still, she inched forward, mesmerized by the power this water, which stretched beyond the horizon, had.

"Amazing, isn't it?" Arie's voice cut through Bridget's thoughts, a warm arm wrapping around hers. "I forgot how big it feels, and how tiny it makes me feel to stand next to it."

"It is." Bridget said, her voice soft, almost inaudible. "I think I want to learn how to swim."

"Yeah?" Arie laughed. "Okay, I'll teach you how to swim. But uh, not here." She hugged Bridget close, then pulled back, staring at the back of Bridget's head.

"What is it?"

"White girl, you are getting one hell of a sunburn."

Bridget touched the back of her neck. Felt the heat of her skin radiating warmth. "I think you're right." She grinned then, thought of her mother standing on this same beach decades before. She thought of how life circles around in the oddest of ways. Annee hadn't wanted to talk about Earth, because she didn't think Bridget would ever see it in person. And why speak of things one can never hope to have?

"Here, get under this. It will help." Arie opened up an umbrella. "The forecast called for rain later. I had the 3D printers print one out."

"Thanks, Arie."

"Always, Bite."

They stood there. As the tide flowed out, the water slowly receded, and the sun slipped lower in the sky behind them. When the sun disappeared, it was time to go. Arie squeezed Bridget into a hug.

"Don't worry, we will come back soon. And we will have a bonfire." Arie said, her frizzy curls bouncing in the moonlight.

Bridget smiled as she stared up at the moon hanging full in the sky. The Shackelton Crater, the closest landmark to her former home, was impossible to see from here, but she knew it was there. The sand had cooled with the setting of the sun and her toes, still damp, were cold. She imagined swimming in this impossibly deep ocean. The thought was terrifying and thrilling at the same time. And in her memories, her mother's voice.

"I see the earth and the earth sees me. Bless the earth and bless me. I see the sun and the sun sees me. Hello sun, how do you be?" Each page on the tablet filled with images of a world Bite never thought she would see. "I see my house and my house sees me. Hello house, were you waiting for me? I see the earth and the earth sees me. Hello earth... will you dream with me?"

"But Annee, the words say moon, not Earth."

And her mother had given her a rare smile. "Well, it fits better this way."

Bite had smiled back at her, "Yes, it does. Always read it that way, okay?"

"What are you thinking 'bout, bestie?" Arie's voice interrupted her musings.

Bridget shrugged, wrapping an arm around her friend. "I see the moon, and the moon sees me."

And Arie looked up at the sky with her, laid her head on Bridget's shoulder, and sighed. "Yes, yes, it does."

Ayomide and Ireti

The Whole Truth

The process had been long. Multiple interviews, a thorough background check, and intrusive questions. Ayomide had endured them all without complaint. After all, sitting in the refugee camps gave her too much time on her hands. Too much time to think of her family, lost to her, thanks to the ESH virus.

The questioning, however, had taken a turn for the worse. The girl, and she was but a slip of a girl, frowned at the tablet in her hand. Ayomide wondered what tiny detail of her life was a problem now. A less than stellar grade in primary school, perhaps? An argument with a neighbor? Had she annoyed someone at the refugee camp or said something wrong?

Her English was flawless, or so she had been told, but occasionally she floundered over the multiple meanings of words. Learning English in a classroom is not the same as speaking it, listening to it, and living it every day. It was a challenge her in this alien place. She missed Nigeria. The smells and sounds were different here, the pace and culture altered, even among other Nigerians. Few were Yoruban and she longed to hear her native language spoken by another voice.

Ayomide sighed, and smoothed her dress, flicking away an errant remnant of leaf. It was fall, and outside the trees were shedding their leaves in a bright and grandiose display of oranges, reds and yellows. It contrasted with the white spires of the new buildings that rose organically from the ashes of the world that was.

"Ms. Batan, I see you were married with two children?"

A flash of memory, the knife in her hand, arcing into Bankole. Too late, too late.

"Yes."

Another frown and the girl glanced up then, meeting Ayomide's gaze. "It says here the children were both AB negative, though."

Ayomide tried to swallow past the lump in her throat. "Yes, they were. My husband was not." She felt her stomach flip, knowing what the girl would ask next, and she dreaded it. Could she refuse to answer? To do so, though, would likely mean returning to the refugee center without a job, without something, anything, to occupy her days. She would have to tell the whole truth, and hope that they wouldn't boot her out of this shiny new office. Worse, out of the refugee center as well. Beneath her brightly colored dress, she felt the sweat build under her armpits. Why had she said "yes" when they asked for Yoruban refugees who had experience with small children? Better to work in a kitchen, far away from children, far away from the reminders of what she had lost. The knife in her hand, the memory so sharp, so painful. And the blood, the loss.

She realized the girl was looking at her. Waiting for her to speak. To explain. Ayomide's chest was tight, her breathing constricted. They would throw her out, maybe even send her back to Nigeria, back to her memories and loss and empty, empty life. But the truth needed to be spoken, so Ayomide sucked a deep breath in and opened her mouth.

With Her Life

Jack looked up at the brisk knock on his open door. Mireille Marcelin stood there, tablet in hand.

"We need to talk about the nanny candidates." She strode into his office, balancing precariously on heels, her stomach round and full. He wasn't sure how she managed walking in the spiky heels with her center of gravity having changed so drastically. But nothing about Mireille could be taken for granted. From her pushes to enact draconian pro-birth legislation to her own fierce dedication to the cause, she was a force of nature.

"Now?" He was in the middle of a disaster. One of the Unaffected Persons cities in South Africa was reporting a potential ESH outbreak. Between that and supply issues on the East coast, along with several reports out of the decaying swamp New York had become, Jack could do with one less issue.

Mireille sat in the seat across from him and said nothing, her fingers flying across her tablet screen. A second later, Jack's tablet beeped with a notification. He looked down at the short list of candidates. The Chairwoman wasn't due to give birth for another month, but it seemed Mireille was determined to tackle the nanny issue now. And who was he to argue with a hormonal pregnant woman? Especially when she was carrying his child.

He suppressed a sigh and focused on the data.

"Ayomide Batan is my first choice." Mireille added, shifting in her seat and grimacing as she placed a hand on her lower back.

Jack opened the file and scanned the record. A pleasant, round-faced woman in traditional African garb smiled up at him. He could see she was currently in one of the refugee camps on the outskirts of New Athens and had been there for nearly four months. Husband deceased. Children, two of them, both deceased. Jack looked back up from the tablet, his shoulders lifting in a shrug.

Mireille raised her eyebrows, pointed at the tablet. "Read the last interview."

Jack suppressed a flash of annoyance. What could be so pressing about a nanny, anyway? He clicked on the links, scanned down the list to the most recent date, and read it. His skin crawled.

"Jesus Christ, Mireille."

"Yeah."

"Why in the hell is she at the top of your list?" Jack said, staring at the words in horror, then back at the beautiful young woman sitting in front of him. "She killed her husband!"

Mireille leaned forward, her brown eyes flashing. "Yes, but look at *why* she did it, Jack. She did it to save her child. It was too late for the boy, but she stopped her husband, a man twice her size. Stronger. Maddened from the ESH virus. But she *stopped* him. And the little girl died two days later at the hospital after a hell of a fight to save her life. Look at the account. She ran with her child for two miles, while wounded, and nearly died herself. She did everything she could to save her child's life. And I believe she will do that for the Chairwoman's baby as well. This woman would protect that baby *with her life*. And after Aiden, isn't that what we need? Someone who will lay down their life in service? She killed her husband, someone she refers to as the love of her life, in order to save her child. That's who we need in the inner circle of the Chairwoman's world."

She leaned back and ticked off the points on her hand.

"Widowed, childless, from Yoruba, just as the sperm donor was, and willing to do whatever is necessary to save the life of a child. She's perfect." Mireille shifted, her left hand rubbing her lower back, a smug, satisfied smile on her face.

Jack shook his head, read the interview again, and tried not to be sick. Ayomide Batan had gone to the grocery store alone, leaving her healthy, ESH-immune children behind with her husband. Only to return and find him having killed their son, partially *consumed* the boy, and also mortally wounded their daughter.

It was the stuff of nightmares.

"Are you sure she's emotionally stable enough? She killed him, for Christ's sake. She *saw* her son partially eaten, and she watched her daughter die. That leaves terrible psychological wounds."

Mireille nodded, her smug smile slipping. "It was the first thing I checked after she told me her story. You will find a full psychological assessment at the bottom. Two actually. She had to pass an initial one just to qualify as a refugee. There's trauma, sure. But if you read the second one, you see that she not only took part in therapy extensively, both before and after she arrived in New Athens, but she has also been working as a grief counselor adjunct to the director of the camp. She had the training prior to marriage and family, and the director credited her with saving five from potential suicides. He wrote that if a full-time counseling position was available, he would place her at the top of the list of candidates. But we already had that well in hand, and Ms. Batan is hoping to find a more positive environment. She worked as a nanny while attending graduate school."

Jack sat back, stroking his chin. The three days growth was still itchy and stubbly. He had always kept it clean-shaven, but after a harrowing three days of one emergency after another, Mireille had told him in no uncertain terms how sexy she found his unkempt face. He had disagreed, and she had insisted on at least a goatee, which he was trying for the sake of peace. Once she latched onto an idea, no amount of arguing would dissuade her. Which was likely the case now, with the nanny position.

"We need at least two more nannies. They need to be available in shifts and allow for days off."

Mireille nodded. "Which is why I've listed eight choices, but the top four are the finalists, and Ayomide is my number one." Her smile disappeared.

"There's something about her, Jack. She's *important*." Her hand stroked her rounded belly. "And she deserves happiness."

"Happiness or love?"

"Both."

"She will be the child's nanny, not her mother." Jack temporized.

"A child can sense if it isn't loved." Mireille fired back. "The nannies I chose will love that baby more than Madeline ever will."

Jack's eyebrows shot up in response. Mireille snorted.

"Come off it, Jack. Madeline isn't the maternal type, and you know it as much as I do. You know I'm right. About the Chairwoman, about Ms. Batan. This baby will need someone who loves it, who would die for it."

"And you think that is Ayomide Batan?"

"I do."

"Fine." Jack reached out and scribbled his signature onto the tablet and pressed Send. "Hire her."

Mireille smiled. "I'll deliver the news myself. I need to swing by that corner of town this afternoon for a few errands." She stood up awkwardly, and Jack's gaze once again fell to her spiky high heels. Mireille winked at him. "I'm not giving them up. It's how you noticed me."

Despite her rounded belly, she made her hips do that sexy sashay and she walked away.

Two Weeks Early

Ayomide was less surprised by the news that they needed her services two weeks early than she was that they wanted her at all. When the notification had flashed across her tablet, she had waited to open up the message until after dinner.

One night a week, she volunteered in the kitchen of the refugee camp. The head chef had asked if there were any special dishes she wanted to share and this had coincided with the rare and heartwarming birth of twins the night before to a fellow Nigerian refugee. Ayomide had carefully reproduced her mother's recipe for Ewa Agoyin, a dish of beans with pepper sauce, edged with plantain. It was received well, especially by her countrymen, and the twins' mother had cried with joy, hugging Ayomide close.

Still, she stared at the notification of the email with trepidation. The little slip of a girl, heavy with child, had come to her at the camp personally two weeks ago, with the offer of the position. She had been clear, however, that it would not be for another month.

Ayomide was still surprised. So sure that she had no chance after having told her story to this young woman clad in expensive clothing who had looked pale and unsettled as she ended the last interview. Ayomide had been certain her chance to watch any child, much less that of the Chairwoman of the Terran United Planetary Government's child, was as dead as her family. Instead, Mireille had offered her the position.

Surely now she had changed her mind. She'd thought about it and found that a woman capable of killing her own husband could never be trusted with a tiny, innocent child. It had been a beautiful fantasy, the thought of holding a child again. But now it was over. Here, alone in her tiny room, the plasteel walls that muted much of the noise outside and held her narrow bunk and a tiny dresser of clothes, here she could grieve this lost chance. Her finger hovered over the open button, interrupted by the device's buzz. An incoming call. She pressed Accept.

"Ms. Batan?" Mireille's familiar voice sounded over the speaker. "Ms. Batan, did you receive my message earlier?"

"No, I was serving dinner." Ayomide answered cautiously. Mireille's tone didn't sound grim. It sounded buoyant, excited.

"Ah, yes, I remember you saying something about that. Well, I'm calling because Madame Chairwoman Chen delivered early, just a few hours ago, and I was hoping you could come in tomorrow instead of in two weeks."

"I..." Ayomide blinked in shock. "Yes, I can be there tomorrow."

"Excellent. I'll send over the information and pass you will need for full access. And since we have all of your other paperwork already completed, there will just be a few signatures and disclosures to do before you can meet little Ireti!"

Hope. The child's name meant hope. In that moment, hope was the overriding emotion that surged through Ayomide. A child to hold and care for and love. Hope. For the world's future. Tears formed in her eyes.

"Thank you, Miss Marcelin." She hoped the girl couldn't hear the warble of emotion in her voice.

"Call me, Mireille, Ms. Batan. I'll see you tomorrow." A soft click and the line disconnected. Ayomide stared at the tablet and sat down slowly on her narrow bed. She started *tomorrow*.

She is Easy to Love

Ireti was tiny, far smaller than either of Ayomide's children had been. Akande, her eldest, had been a hefty four kilograms, while Ade had slid quietly into the world at just over three kilograms. Ireti couldn't weigh over two and a half. The nurse, a petite, dark-haired and olive-skinned woman, had watched over the tiny baby for what felt like a long time, as Ayomide shifted the tiny newborn in her arms and fed her a bottle of breastmilk. They stocked the refrigerator with bottles and bottles of it. More than could have come from Chairwoman Chen. Ayomide had overheard the nurses discussing it. Her milk hadn't come in, and even if it did, no one was sure she would have enough production to keep up. Hence the banked breast milk. Women were losing babies in record numbers, even late term, and sometimes they encouraged the grieving mothers to pump in order to give a precious gift to those few babies who survived. The stores of breast milk were growing faster than the demand.

Ireti's skin was paler than Ayomide's. She examined the newborn's tiny fist, closed tight around her pointer finger. Her skin was the color of coffee with a generous addition of cream, whereas Ayomide's was that of dark toffee. Not surprising considering the Chairwoman looked more like bone china, and just as translucent. Ireti had a voracious appetite, however, and Ayomide could not help but smile as the tiny infant made quick work of the bottle and then, with gentle encouragement, burped. The smell of sweet milk wafted through the air.

Ayomide's mouth hurt from smiling. Holding this tiny baby, this vessel of unimaginable potential set at the beginning of a hopefully long and happy life, was exactly what she had needed. It was overwhelming. She had spent almost a week with Ireti, holding her, singing to her, feeding and caring for her. And the smile stayed. Even as tears ran down her face. Memories of her two beautiful children, of their laughter and love and giggles, washing over her. *Ireti is not your child*, she reminded herself at intervals. But it was easy to forget when the hours stretched between visits from Chairwoman Chen.

Madeline Chen had given birth, spent a mere two days recovering, and then returned to work, visiting once in the morning and once in the evening, every day. And with her, a handful of advisers by her side, vying for her attention.

Ayomide found her initial nerves at meeting the leader of Earth faded in the face of Madeline's smile. The fiery-haired woman had a backbone of steel, but she was also kind. She didn't speak down to Ayomide, and moved with grace whenever she entered the nursery. Ireti, already bonding to Ayomide, shifted restlessly in her mother's arms whenever Madeline Chen held her fussing. It was as if the infant sensed Madeline was unmoored by her and the mysterious status of motherhood. The visits grew shorter and shorter.

Ayomide reveled in the position she held. Yes, she shared it with others, and yes, they were kind and wonderful women, all of them, but there was something about her time with Ireti that nothing else compared to. When she left her and went back to her small apartment in the south wing, a spacious place provided as part of her position, she struggled with what to do with herself in her off-hours. She wanted to hold Ireti close. To smell her sweet, cloying baby smell.

There was a spot, right near the soft fontanel, the opening in the skull that all babies have, that she would press her nose gently against. If she could sit there, unmoving, and just breathe that beautiful scent in for hours, the day would be perfection.

In time, hours would go by with no interruption. Outside of the nursery doors, here in the inner seat of power, laws were being created, rebellions squashed, and the future of humanity hung in the balance. But inside of the nursery, all of that faded away. It was simply the two of them inside of a suite of rooms dedicated to harmony, peace, and love. Soft blankets, lighting that was never harsh or blinding, and the sound of Ayomide's voice singing her charge to sleep kept the outside world at bay.

Even the news of the monstrous asteroid, Azrael, hurtling toward Earth, threatening to destroy the ragtag remnants of humanity, could not break her free from the simple joy of caring for Ireti.

Ayomide knew that the Chairwoman's child would be spirited to safety long before disaster struck. And as she rocked the little baby to sleep, nothing past Ireti's own survival mattered to her. The other nannies fretted, worried, but they still had ties to the world. Friends. Even family. Ayomide had nothing and no one past Ireti. She wasn't standoffish, nor even really against making connections with others, not at all. It was simply that she existed for one person, and one person alone. Ireti.

She is so easy to love. What more could I ask for in this world?

Weeks. Months. More than a year had gone by. Her feelings remained the same. And Ireti clung to her, smiled like the sun when she arrived in the morning, and babbled happily at her all day.

Ayomide was singing Ireti's favorite song, the song Ayomide's own children had loved, when Madeline Chen entered the room one afternoon.

Nitori l'otito ni wura

Iyebiye ti ko ṣee ṣe pataki

Eyi ti o ntan ati didan

Ni awọn ọjọ ti o ṣokunkun julọ ti igbesi aye

Tutu awọn irora wa ti o jinlẹ julọ

Idaduro wa lailewu nipasẹ awọn iji lile ti igbesi aye

Ki a le tàn ninu goolu gara

Ireti was smiling broadly at Ayomide. She loved the song. Ireti didn't seem to care that her mother had come into the nursery. In fact, she barely noticed Madeline was there. She focused all of her being on the song. Her body swayed in time to Ayomide's singing, her tiny fingers kept a beat of sorts.

It surprised Ayomide to see Madeline. It was the middle of the day, and it was unusual for the Chairwoman to visit at this time of day. This was good, since Ireti had just woken from a quick nap. She would have been fussy just an hour before. Ayomide felt torn between continuing to hold the little girl and sing as the toddler wanted, or breaking routine and acknowledging that the child's mother had entered the room. Better to recognize her, she decided. She pointed to the Chairwoman, "Ireti, your iya, your mama, is here to see you!" She smiled at Madeline and bowed her head in a sign of respect. "Ma'am."

"The song you were singing, Ayomide, it was lovely." Madeline reached out and tried to caress Ireti's hair. Ayomide flushed in embarrassment as Ireti turned away and buried her tiny head in Ayomide's chest.

"She just woke up and is still tired. I am sorry, ma'am." Ayomide's anxiety flared, and she watched the Chairwoman's hand drop away.

"No, no, it is nothing. Don't worry, Ayomide, she feels safe with you, and that is good. It is as it should be."

"It is a Yoruba lullaby," Ayomide said, returning to Madeline's question, one hand stroking Ireti's back. "Mother is gold, a treasure untold," she said and then hummed the song again under her breath.

Madeline sat down on the couch. "It's lovely. I can see that Ireti likes it."

"She is a wonderful baby, ma'am. I so enjoy my time with her. Would you like to hold her?"

"When she is ready, yes. But for now, she looks content in your arms, Ayomide. Tell me," the Chairwoman asked, "what does your name mean?"

"My name?" Ayomide smiled. "It means 'when joy returns.' I was the only girl after five boys and my mother was so thrilled. She finally had the girl she was hoping for."

"Ireti means hope, as I imagine you know already."

"Yes," Ayomide said, nodding, "very appropriate."

"Did you have children before, Ayomide?"

She paused from rubbing Ireti's back and nodded slowly. "Yes, ma'am, I had two children. One boy, Akande, and a girl, Ade. They died with their father early in the outbreak. The children were both immune, as I was, but their father was not. My Bankole was a good man, kind and patient, but the virus turned him into something I could not recognize." She paused, gently gathered Ireti, and handed her to Madeline before continuing.

"I think about that day often. What I could have done different. Had I known what would happen, how the hunger would overtake him, I would have sent him out to the store instead. Or taken our sweet children with me." She stared at her empty hands. "But I didn't take them with me, or send him out for food. I didn't do that."

Ireti sat calmly in Madeline's arms. She reached up and touched Madeline's face.

"She is perfect. Exactly what my aching heart has needed," Ayomide said. "It is so easy to love her."

"Yes," Madeline echoed, "Babies are so easy to love."

The Chairwoman didn't react as Ireti slid from her arms and crawled away from both women to play with a ball on the floor. And later, as Madeline Chen left the nursery, her daughter barely noticed her departure.

Ayomide sighed, partly in relief, but also in sadness. For Madeline Chen, who despite leading the entire world, seemed hopeless at connecting with her own flesh and blood. And Ayomide sighed also for herself, reminding herself yet again. *She is not your child.*

Ayomide could not help thinking of how Ireti's face lit up in the morning when Ayomide came in and took over for the evening shift, a cheerful, round-faced young woman who had suffered two miscarriages, one late term, in the past year. It was Ayomide that Ireti gravitated to and bonded closest with. It was Ayomide who felt her heart leap with every smile, every slobbery toddler kiss. She loved this child. More than she should. No matter that every morning and every evening, she told herself the same five words she had said from the beginning. *She is not your child.* It didn't matter. Heart and soul, she loved Ireti, and she knew the little girl felt the same way. Madeline was a mother in name only.

Slowly, that reminder was changing to the question, always the question. *What will Ireti do when I am gone?*

Reading of the Names

Ayomide kissed Ireti good night, waited until the little girl's eyes had grown heavy with sleep, and slowly stole away, closing the nursery door behind her as she left. Her room was just next door, a sharp departure from the large and rather empty apartment she had occupied in the south wing. She had left it a year ago, shortly after a spate of unrest, which had included the loss of two of the nanny team members. One to childbirth, one to suicide. It had been Chairwoman Chen who suggested it, and Ayomide had not questioned. She'd been far too happy at the turn of events to argue. A chance to be with Ireti more? Absolutely. Now, the only time they were apart was on her days off. The other nanny, Deirdre, was content to work part-time now that she was remarried and she and her husband were busy trying for a child. They already had won coveted space in the Cheyenne Mountain Complex shortly after the reading of the names. Both were young, with years of potential fertility in front of them, should the nanite research currently rumored to be in final testing become effective and reverse the damage wrought by the ESH virus.

A spot of tea and then off to bed. Ireti had been waking earlier in the morning as she edged closer to her third birthday. Ayomide's hand had closed on the hot water kettle in the small kitchenette when a soft knock came at the door, followed by it gliding open.

Ayomide blinked in surprise. "Madame Chairwoman, good evening."

Madeline smiled briefly and looked about the room. "Is she...?"

"Already asleep, ma'am. I could wake her if you would like, or..."

Madeline waved a hand. "No, no, I was hoping to speak with you alone, Ayomide. If you don't mind."

Ayomide's heart skipped a beat, and she felt sick. Now would be when the Chairwoman came to tell her she was no longer needed. That Ireti would leave on a starship to Mars, safely tucked in Cryo, to sleep while Earth died. *She is not your child.* No matter how many times she told herself that, it didn't matter. She felt how she felt.

"Is it time for Ireti to go into Cryo?" she asked, her fingers still clutching the teapot. Madeline's eyes focused on the teapot.

"Would you mind if we had some tea and discussed what happens next?" Madeline said, her tone kind, as if she were speaking to a friend.

"Of course. I was about to make a Nigerian tea. It is, how do you say, like, hm, hot chocolate? It is Ireti's favorite drink."

Madeline smiled warmly. "I would like that, yes."

Ayomide set the water pot to boil and retrieved the evaporated milk from the refrigerator and the Milo from the cabinet. She poured the concoction together in two mugs and handed one to Madeline, who was examining a drawing Ireti had made of Ayomide that morning.

"Thank you." Madeline accepted the steaming mug from Ayomide, and they both sat down at the round kitchen table. She gestured toward the drawing. "She is improving. Such detail!"

Ireti had spent nearly thirty minutes focusing on Ayomide's dress - a predominantly purple satin with red piping and gold sleeves. She smiled, thinking of Ireti's determination to capture her likeness just so. "She is very talented, Madame Chairwoman."

"Call me Madeline, Ms. Batan."

"Only if you will call me Ayomide, ma'am."

They shared a smile, as if it were a secret, and sipped their tea for a moment in silence.

"You withdrew your name from consideration, Ayomide. I wanted to know why."

Ayomide hid her surprise by staring at her teacup. It was a moment before she could summon the words. When she did, they came out as a whisper.

"When Ireti boards the ship for Mars, I will have nothing left here on Earth. There are others far more deserving of a future than myself."

"Have you considered how Ireti would feel, Ayomide?"

Ayomide could not meet the Chairwoman's eyes. As it was, they were quickly filling with tears. The thought of saying goodbye to her... *she is NOT your child...* to Madeline's child, was breaking her heart.

"She will have her mother to watch over her, ma'am."

There was a tap at the door. Madeline stood abruptly, her tea sloshing over the side of the cup. She strode to the door and opened it. One of her aides, a tall, grim-faced man, stood on the other side. He handed her a thin tablet. "Thank you, Jack. That will be all for tonight."

"Yes, ma'am." He glanced at Ayomide with an inscrutable expression before the door shut. Madeline returned to the table, the tablet glowing in her hand. She set it down next to Ayomide's tea cup and pushed it closer to her.

"I'll need you to read this, Ayomide." She settled down in the seat, reached for a napkin, and wiped absently at the spilled tea before taking a sip. "This is lovely tea. I wish I had gotten to try it sooner. I think I'd prefer it over coffee any day."

Ayomide barely heard the Chairwoman's words. Her eyes, having blinked away the tears, stared at the words on the tablet in confusion and shock. She reached out, paged through it, and gasped. The documents before her they made no sense.

Articles of adoption.

Official birth certificate for Ireti Batan

Assignment to the Masa Depan Bumi lifeship for Ayomide and Ireti Batan

Moments passed. Ayomide paged through the documents, then returned and paged through them again.

"I... I don't, I don't understand."

Madeline sipped the tea. "Ayomide," she said softly, "*you* are a mother." She reached for her wedding ring, a large marquise cut antique behemoth that hung loose on her right ring finger. "Gary never wanted children. Truth be told, neither did I. My sister had three, you know." She laughed. It was short, aborted. "My sister was one of those super moms. House, children, business - everything perfect. She could do it all. But me, I was a politician's wife. I was good at it, too. I never felt that 'tick, tick, tick' of the biological clock women talk about. Never."

She stood up, her long, slender legs carrying her about the room in a random, nervous pattern. Ayomide realized that even now, no part of the Chairwoman could be still or quiet. It wasn't in her DNA.

"I followed the advice of my advisers. And it was good advice. It was! Millions of women looked to me as a beacon for change. The opportunity to rebuild our civilization, to show them motherhood, was what we needed in these dark, terrible days. And Ireti is beautiful and sweet and so smart." She stopped then, staring once again at the carefully rendered colors of Ayomide's dress in Ireti's drawing. She turned and Ayomide saw a flash of regret, sadness in her eyes.

"But it is you she loves, Ayomide. I gave birth to her, yes. But I'm not her mother. You are." She sighed then. "Sign the document. Please. Sign it and you and your daughter will board the lifeship in two days."

Ayomide shook her head, tears welling in her eyes. "You don't know what I did, ma'am. To my... to my husband. If you did, you would never have..."

Madeline interrupted her with a sharp bark of laughter. "Of course I know, Ayomide. You tried to save your child from a terrible death. I read about how you ran with her in your arms, fended off attacks by others maddened with the ESH virus, and got her to the hospital. You did everything you could to protect your child. Just as you will do everything in your power to protect Ireti. A child I know you love. Did you really think I wouldn't know exactly who was caring for her? When Jack showed me the report and told me Mireille had picked you, he didn't understand, but I did. I knew Ireti deserved someone who would do *anything* to keep her safe. And you will do it, just as you will love her, more than anyone else. What more could I ask for? Biology aside, Ayomide, she *is* your child."

Masa Depan Bumi

The next two days had passed in a blur. The documents, signed, and filed so they were legally binding. Madeline Chen had come the last night of Ayomide's and Ireti's stay on Earth and said goodbye to her child.

"You are going on a grand adventure, child. But Ayomide will be by your side." She didn't explain beyond that, and Ireti didn't ask. It was only after Madeline turned away that Ireti had run to her and given her a hug goodbye, surprising them both.

The day was sunny and beautiful. There was nothing in the sky that so much as hinted toward the destruction to come. The day was cloudless and blue.

Ayomide held Ireti's hand in hers. The anonymity of it all felt surreal. At three, Ireti had rarely seen beyond the walls of the Chairwoman's residence. Her face, always blurred on the feeds to protect her privacy, was mostly unknown. And here they stood, Ireti's body nestled close against her, anxious at the change in routine and the growling in her small belly. No meals after midnight so that Cryo didn't have an unexpected deleterious effect on her tiny body.

"Iya?"

"Yes, love?"

"Will I dream?"

Ayomide considered this for a moment. Ireti's hair was pulled back in a simple set of neat braids. Her little brown eyes stared up at her with a mixture of apprehension and excitement.

"I do not know."

Ireti looked pensive. "If we dream, I want us to have the same dream. I think that would be very nice."

Ayomide felt a smile stretch her lips wide. "Yes, that would."

The line moved forward and Ayomide looked around at the city spires in the distance, and the massive lifeship that stood before them now. This world had seen so much death. It would see more. It would see destruction. The seas would boil, and hellfire would rain down from above. Despite this, she felt hope. Hope for the years that would follow. Ireti's hand clasped in hers. Her future, their future, stood waiting millions of miles away. And she would do everything in her power to give her child the best future possible.

At the Gates

08.09.2104
New Athens

Empty City

New Athens wasn't as empty as he would have expected. As Jeff walked down the broad, clean street, his back to the now-empty TUPG headquarters, he could still see pockets of people here and there. Some were scurrying to the transportation hubs, baggage in hand, queuing up to catch the last transports out to the designated safe zones. But there were far too many others who moved slowly, as if out for a stroll, as if the world wasn't about to undergo a bombardment unheard of in millions of years. He marveled at that. Were they actually staying? They couldn't actually believe they would be safe here, could they?

New Athens was well within the destruction zone. Not the initial meteor strikes, of course, but the tsunami that would wash over the city from the south would wipe clean the land he was currently walking. None of the structures would survive according to the impact prediction models. All of their hard work in creating this beautiful city. An intentional, planned, and perfectly executed city, and it would all be swept away as if it had never existed.

Behind him stood the seat of power. Inside of the chambers, marked by the tall white spires, he had stood by Madeline Chen's side for the past four years, helping her, arguing with her, and now, she was gone. Not to the lifeship with her daughter and nanny, as expected. Not to the Cheyenne Mountain Complex, where a suite of rooms awaited him and a handful of other members of her team. Madeline had inexplicably chosen to stay behind. To meet her fate when Azrael fell to Earth. There was still so much work to do, to help restart humanity, but the Chairwoman wanted nothing of it.

"Live, Jeff. Take your place in Cheyenne. Find someone special. Make a life in the world to come." She had said to him. "Imagine the impact you could have in a world washed clean of sin, of hubris, free of these terrible choices I made."

No matter what he had said or argued, her mind seemed made up. How late had he argued with her last night? Late enough that he was insensible, deeply dreaming as she slipped from her suite of rooms in the early morning hours, leaving only a note penned for him behind.

It is time for you to go to Cheyenne, Jeff. Don't disappoint me.

The flitter waited. Keyed to his biometrics, the slender, one-seater sat in a nearby parking lot waiting for him to arrive. He slung the bag over his shoulder and headed for the lot, unease permeating every part of him.

This isn't how the story should end.

He slid into the flitter and stared at the sky, watching for the first signs of Azrael to appear as the sleek machine executed a quick turn and ascended.

"How long until arrival, NARA?" He asked the onboard computer.

"One hour, seven minutes until arrival in Cheyenne, Wyoming's airspace."

Jeff Bonovich sighed, and watched as the city fell away, replaced by trees and empty stretches of land far, far below.

Chaos and Desperation

Where New Athens had been calm, ordered, serene - the scene outside the Cheyenne Mountain Complex was anything but. It began with a long line of vehicles which snaked down the mountain for miles. Jeff could see it clearly from his eagle-eye view in the flitter as it began its descent. And not just vehicles, but hundreds, no, thousands of people on foot, carrying bags, children, even dogs and cats. Desperate people with nowhere to go, nowhere to hide from the chaos that would soon rain down upon them.

The flitter leveled out, slowing, and Jeff realized it was slowly circling.

"NARA, status?"

"There is an unexpected delay. All landings are on temporary hold." NARA's voice was unruffled, calm. As the flitter circled again, Jeff could see that the people on the road were but a small part of the mass crowd gathered near the gates. There had to be thousands of them. How would he ever get through? A part of him wanted to order NARA back to New Athens, back to the quiet city.

He could join the others there who had either accepted their fate or were in denial. Perhaps the impact predictions would be wrong, the city safe.

"I have an update." NARA interrupted his thoughts. "We are being re-routed to a landing position inside of the perimeter. Arrival in three minutes, fifteen seconds."

The flitter's position adjusted, and he could see a new section, hidden by a small rise in the ground, with yet another crowd isolated behind tall gates. The crowd was smaller, but the people looked just as desperate. Just beyond it, a large helipad. He watched as the mass of bodies resolved into faces staring at him from the far side of the fence. Most of them looked terrified. A few openly glared. The flitter gently landed on the center of the helipad and a pair of heavily armed soldiers approached.

The taller one waited for the flitter door to open. "Sir? Your access credentials, please."

Jeff reached for the badge that hung around his neck. The soldier nodded and pointed to the stone edifice several hundred feet away.

"Right this way, sir. They will have your assigned space at the entrance."

The noise from the crowd drew Jeff's attention. He would have to walk right by this group. Near the front, he could see a rather familiar looking young man. Where had he seen him before? Beside him was a young woman with a shaved head on one side and dreadlocks on the other. Her eyes, though, her eyes of fire bored into his. A creche baby. Here.

"Who are these people? Why are they separated from the others?" Jeff asked the soldiers.

The shorter one shrugged. "Partials."

"Partials?"

"Couples where one has access, the other doesn't." The man replied, "They are waiting to see if anyone already guaranteed a spot doesn't show up. Otherwise, the only one we can let in is the one on the approved list."

This wasn't supposed to happen like this. The lottery had considered relationship status and families.

Jeff's gaze connected with the young man's. Damned if he didn't know that kid. He struggled to place his face.

"Sir, if you could please proceed to Intake, we need this space clear."

"Right, right." Jeff forced his body into motion. The small wheeled autocase followed close.

As one of the higher echelon, he could have brought more belongings. That morning, he had stared at the contents of his apartment and back at the two empty autocases waiting to be filled. He stared at a small geode collection he had carefully collected since adolescence, the handful of rare fossils his paleontologist mother had passed down to him when she passed away from a rare form of leukemia ten years ago, and considered adding them to his meager set of belongings. He had his entire life of photos and vids encoded on a palm-size viewer, a bizarre Hawaiian shirt a former lover had given him, and a fistful of ancient marbles found in and around his great-grandmother's ancient brick home in Pennsylvania.

None of it mattered. He had left it all. Someday, if man actually survived the onslaught of Azrael and the tsunamis and the long asteroid-induced decade of winter, perhaps someone would find his treasure trove. Perhaps he would return to find it right here, just as he had left it.

He walked toward the stone-carved entrance. As it closed in around him, he felt a dread wash over him. He didn't belong here, and he certainly didn't deserve to be here. He had no one and nothing.

The entrance to Cheyenne Mountain Complex was a long walk. Around him, the mountain leaned in close. The whitewashed walls felt oppressive, heavy. The further he walked, the slower his steps were. How could he stay in a place like this for a decade or more? What if the world never recovered, and they were trapped down here, doomed to live out their days beneath this mountain of rock? The thought of it was horrifying.

Ahead was a well-lit space. The massive blast doors were at least two, possibly three feet thick, the opening wide and high enough to accommodate large trucks loaded to the gills with supplies. The trucks were gone now, their jobs complete, but the blast doors stood open, ready to receive the last refugees.

Jeff had watched the footage while the endless array of deliveries had come through, including several thousand people who would never walk the halls nor eat the food. They had loaded their Cryo tubes into the depths of the cave system, far underneath what would become the working government here on Earth. They stationed a battalion of soldiers armed to the teeth at intervals. There would be no chaos here, no allowing unapproved refugees sanctuary. If the vast crowds outside of the gates were to break through, which they couldn't, they would never make it past the soldiers' guns.

They staffed the desk with a handful of civilians. Several sat typing on their tablets, another couple were on headsets getting status updates. A woman in the center of the table motioned him forward. "Representative Bonovich?"

Jeff nodded.

"Let the floor coordinator know that the last member of the government has arrived," she told the young man with a headset seated next to her. He nodded and murmured her message into his headset. She turned back to Jeff. "You are in Section I on the third level." She peered over at his autocase, eyebrows raised. "Is that all of your belongings? If you need help with any other items, I can get someone to help."

He shook his head. "No, this is it."

"Well," she laughed, "Don't you travel light!"

He thought of the young man he had seen outside. So familiar, so...

"Tobias Aaronson." The kid's name had suddenly popped into his head. The adopted son of Julie Lynn Aaronson, one of leaders of the team that had limited success with the artificial wombs. Her wife, Janelle Brooks, and Janelle's adopted daughter had boarded the lifeship bound for Mars after Dr. Aaronson's death. Was the fire-eyed woman by his side the reason he hadn't joined his adoptive family in the lifeship?

She blinked. "I beg your pardon?"

"Outside at the gate. With a young woman. Can you check to see if he is on the list?"

She blinked, typed the name and frowned. "Aaronson, Tobias. He's a geneticist and yes, he is on the list. You said he was with someone?"

"Yes, a young woman." Jeff straightened. Her eyes had been odd, disconcerting. Her face was familiar as well now that he thought about it. She had made a personal appeal to Madeline. She and another one of her kind. All born from artificial wombs, the failed promise to become the mothers of a new generation. They were all infertile, according to the researchers' reports. "She's from the artificial wombs project."

The distaste on the woman's face was immediate. "I can assure you that... girl is not on the list. Abominations, and infertile. They have no place in Cheyenne's sanctuary."

A soldier near the massive set of doors muttered loud enough for Jeff to hear. "Thank God that thing isn't allowed in. Got a look at her eyes when I was coming in. Ain't normal."

So that was why Tobias was outside. Somehow, he had connected with one of his mother's surviving creations. Near the doors was a large screen. It moved from camera to camera set around the Cheyenne Mountain Complex. The common areas inside, where figures moved with purpose, small bots humming along by their sides. The views of outside, the crowds, the desperate cries of the doomed were unheard, but easily imagined. He could see their mouths moving, a mother offering her baby to a soldier, her face awash with tears. And always, in the top right corner of the screen, was the countdown to Armageddon. The end of their world. Jeff had watched it move from years to months, then days, and now, finally, hours. All he had to do was walk through those giant blast doors. These people, they told him he belonged here. They had made a space. Accommodations. Rations. A life was waiting here.

Stay and survive, or live for whatever time I have left. I can suck off of my position one last time or go find Madeline.

The woman at the desk said something. Her mouth moved. Words came out, but all he could hear were the silent screams of the crowd on the screen before him.

He thought of the note Madeline had left him. The delicate swirls of cursive, a rare and dying art of writing. *It is time for you to go to Cheyenne, Jeff. Don't disappoint me.* In his mind's eye, he could see Tobias Aaronson's face, partially obscured by the tall iron gates. Tobias was out there instead of in here. Why? Likely for much of the same reason that Jeff had spent the last four years of his life by Madeline Chen's side. *Why am I here? When I could be by her side right now?*

Jeff spun on his heel.

"Sir? Representative Bonovich? Sir?" the woman called out behind him. He walked faster, eager to escape this tomb of stone, suddenly desperate for the fresh air he had left behind. He knew where he needed to be. And it wasn't in Cheyenne.

My Life for Yours

Tobias and the woman had shifted in the crowd. No longer in front, and Jeff felt a jolt of fear run through him. Were they gone? Had the soldiers sent them back to the massive throng further back outside of the outer perimeter? He would never find them if they were gone from here. His memories suddenly pulled up the first time he had seen the boy, years ago, with his adopted sister. They had held the tiny infant with the fiery eyes in their arms, looking awkward, unaccustomed to their surroundings in the massive, white-spired hall of the new capitol.

Later, a teen. Just a fleeting glimpse of the boy at Dr. Aaronson's celebration of life, days after her death. A solemn look on Tobias' face as he described Julie helping him to his feet in a refugee camp and taking him under her wing. Hadn't the boy said he was studying genetics? Tobias Aaronson *needed* to be inside of Cheyenne. He had a place in the world to come. Not Jeff.

His autocase followed him obediently as he strode towards the tall gates that held the smaller crowd of hopefuls. The soldiers he spoke to upon arrival were nowhere in sight, and as he drew closer to the gates, a tall, red-haired soldier stopped him.

"Sir, please step back from the gates."

Jeff's gaze dropped to the soldier's name sewn onto his uniform. "Evers? I'm looking for Tobias Aaronson and his companion. They were here a few moments ago." He raised his voice to carry over the noise of the crowd, which had grown since he had first arrived.

"Sir, I need you to return to Intake, please." Evers replied, forcing Jeff back a step.

Jeff steeled himself. "No."

"Sir, I have orders."

"You have orders to maintain this crowd, Evers. To ensure that the right people get into the mountain safely before Azrael comes for us all." Jeff said, his spine straightening. "And I guarantee you, I do not belong in Cheyenne." He glimpsed Tobias out of the corner of his eye. Behind him, the tall girl with the eyes of fire. "That young man right there belongs inside and I'm handing that young woman right there my place inside."

He reached for his badge, whipping it off of his head. "Let them through, and I will take my leave of this place."

Inside, the self-preservation side of him was gibbering in fear. He would die. And for what? For who? But he could see it then. He saw it in their eyes as Evers stopped trying to herd him back into the mountain and instead, inexplicably, turned toward the gate.

Evers turned back to Jeff. "Are you officially requesting Plan B, sir?"

Jeff smiled. Plan B was announced the day following Madeline's speech before the Reading of the Names in which every citizen of the Terran United Planetary Government had received notice of whether they would have a chance at survival on a lifeship or in the sanctuary spaces deep underground. Plan B was an addendum he had pushed forward to ensure some level of choice given to those selected to survive. With it, had come a wave of petitioners who elected to have their children, grandchildren, lovers, and more allowed in, at the price of their own lives.

Jeff ignored the gibbering fear of death rising in him. *Everyone dies. Let mine mean something.* "Yes, I officially request Plan B for..." he paused, not knowing the young woman's name.

Tobias pulled her from behind him and gave her a gentle push forward, towards the edge of the gates. Jeff looked her over. She was whip-thin, yet graceful. She covered her arms in tattoos, including one on her arm that portrayed a mechanical arm hiding beneath the skin. Was that how she thought of herself? Jeff couldn't help but wonder. As something that only pretended to be human? Or was it simply how she had been treated by those far more ignorant?

Even with his sacrifice, her road inside would not be easy. He remembered the women at the Intake desk. They saw her as less than human. Just because she hadn't developed in a human womb. The boy's hand was upon hers, a look of tenderness and love on his face. Tobias found her worthy of love and devotion. If this young man could see it, then hopefully others could as well.

"Syn Travani."

Of course. The first group born of the creche babies, her and her sisters' growth artificially sped up - turned into adults in just over four years - a medical miracle. And one that Dr. Aaronson and Dr. Brooks, Tobias' adoptive mothers, had made happen.

"Syn Travani. I wish to transfer all rights and my place in the Cheyenne Mountain Sanctuary to Syn Travani." Jeff said, his voice ringing over the crowd. There would be no mistaking it, no misunderstanding.

The soldier, Evers, nodded to a young woman in fatigues. She brought over a tablet, her fingers danced across the screen briefly, and she extended it towards Jeff.

"If you could please provide the biometric data here, Sir."

Jeff pressed his thumb against the bioreader, then signed his name. The gate opened, and the crowd shuffled and repositioned as Tobias and Syn were brought into the inner circle, their salvation just a few hundred yards away.

Tobias stepped forward, clasped Jeff's hands in his. "Thank you."

Syn did the same. Jeff felt her hand in his. Human. As human as he was. As human as any of them.

"Live well, Syn Travani." He said, then stepped back, and walked away from them to the flitter he had abandoned on the helipad. A squeak of tire across the ground revealed his trusty autocase still following him about. He stopped outside of the flitter, unzipped the case and pulled out the raucous Hawaiian shirt he had packed inside of it. The past four years had been nothing but suits, neutral colors, and blandness. He was still buttoning the shirt as the flitter rose into the air.

Instead, I will take my place by the sea and watch the Angel of Death descend on the planet and the people I have pledged to serve. I will make my stand and accept the fate that so many of you will share with me. I will be strong. And I ask you to be strong as well.

He knew exactly where she was. She had once told him of the beach that was a short walk from her childhood home.

"NARA, set a course for Half Moon Bay, California."

NARA beeped, "Course set. Anticipated arrival in 32 minutes."

Toes in the Sand

He'd arrived in 47 minutes, having detoured at the last minute in Half Moon Bay itself. Shuttered, nearly empty. He had spoken to no one as he collected the various supplies. And now, as the flitter landed a hundred yards from the shoreline on the gloomy beach, he could see a familiar figure standing in the distance. At the horizon beyond, he had seen the fireball enter the atmosphere. Azrael was here. He tried to remember what the scientists had said about it, about how long it would take for the giant wall of seawater to rise into the sky and annihilate anything within a hundred miles or more of shore.

An hour? Two? He wasn't sure. It didn't matter. All that mattered was here, standing near the shore, digging her toes into the sand.

She was wearing a pale blue dress. A tad bit cold for the day, and stark contrast to her trademark suit. She was so intent on watching the water and the sky, Madeline hadn't even noticed his arrival.

"Mind a little company?" Jeff asked. He reached down and stripped off his shoes and socks and tossed them into a bundle of seaweed. It was growing darker, storm clouds already scudding about in the distance. "I think you picked the wrong beach for viewing the end of the world."

Madeline looked at him with a mixture of shock and dismay. "You had a space, I made sure of it."

"Yeah, well, there was this crazy, tattooed, dread-locked girl with fiery eyes at the gates and her smart-mouthed teenage boyfriend determined to get her in. True love, what could I do?" Jeff said, digging his toes into the sand. "You know, I can't remember how long it has been since I dug my toes in the sand."

"Jeff..."

"Madeline..."

Grief twisted her face.

"You need to live, Jeff. Of all the people... you are one of the good ones. You, Jack, Aiden." Her voice cracked when she said the last name. Losing Aiden had been a blow to all of them. In so many ways, Aiden had been the heart of their team. "You shouldn't be here."

Jeff leaned down, scooped up a handful of sand, and watched as it ran through his fingers, coating them with a fine layer. "I think I'm exactly where I need to be." He reached into the pack slung over his right shoulder. "I even brought snacks. Contraband. Hell, I even brought a couple of doses of Danake if we don't want to wait for the wave." He pulled out a cellophane-wrapped bag of Twinkies, wiggling his eyebrows as he did.

She laughed, even as the tears ran down her cheeks.

"I even found some Twix. Some damned factory has been generating junk food for the past few months and I can't help but indulge. My A1C is likely through the roof." He tossed one towards her and she caught it.

"I didn't think they even made these old candies anymore. Not after the Healthy Bodies Act." Madeline stared at the Twix in her hand, a mix of guilt and longing on her face.

Jeff grinned. "Take a bite."

"I haven't eaten something this sugar-filled in more than a decade."

"All the more reason." He nudged her hand, and she unwrapped the Twix and bit into the bar, her eyes closing as she chewed and swallowed the sweet treat.

"Cue the diabetic coma," she said wryly.

"I think that, somewhere along the way of trying to save humanity, we forgot what it means to live," Jeff said, biting into the Twinkie.

"So, junk food is what it means to live?"

He raised his eyebrows, smiled, and gestured around them. "Look at where we are, Madeline. Here, where you grew up. Your fondest memories, perhaps. A simple beach, with sand and surf, and the salt air. Tell me your eight-year-old self wouldn't have wanted this, along with a Twinkie," he said as he handed the second one over. "And a sandcastle. We have to have a sandcastle."

"You want to build a sandcastle?" she asked him, a bemused smile on her face.

"Yeah. I really do."

Hours later, a wonky sandcastle stood near the edge of the surf. "I remember being better at this," Madeline said, brushing the sand from her knees.

"Well, it's my first sandcastle. So, I think we did great." Jeff winked at her.

Hold My Hand

The wind suddenly picked up and did not fade, snatching away their breaths and the future.

The moment between them vanished as the surf, so close to the edge of the sandcastle, now fled at an alarming rate, racing down the beach. The edges of rocks, a sharp drop-off they hadn't seen, suddenly exposed, and fish and other sea creatures littered the way, caught off-guard by the sudden disappearance of the sea. They could see a black wall of water forming in the distance.

"Azrael..." Madeline whispered. "Jeff, I tore apart families. Forced women to have babies they didn't want. Took their right to choose away from them."

Jeff reached for her hand. Her fingers were icy, coated with sand. "I've told no one this. Once, when I was twelve, I stole a neighbor kid's bike. I stole it and I never gave it back."

Madeline choked and laughed. "Hoodlum."

"Fascist."

He gripped her hand tighter. "Time for our souls to be weighed."

In the far distance, lightning flashed, illuminating a massive darkness rising higher and higher into the sky, roiling black clouds combined with ink-black ocean water until there was little distinction between where the sky ended and the water began. The light breeze was now a gale-force wind that snatched their words away. It didn't matter. Nothing mattered any longer.

He realized then, in that small and great moment, how much he loved her, and always had. A woman both delicate and beautiful, as well as strong and brave. She had made the hard decisions, and he had fought her on so many of them. They had battled, much as lovers might battle, knowing without a doubt that they are in the right.

He hadn't known, never would, the feel of her body wrapped in his. It didn't matter. Nothing mattered but this moment, in this space and time.

They had survived the ESH virus. They had survived upheaval, assassination attempts, and riots. But they would not survive this.

"I love you, Madeline." His lips moved, but the roar of the wind, the growl of the black wall of water moving towards them with such unbelievable speed and darkness, ate the words. Perhaps she heard. She clung harder to his hand, her eyes closed, and he thought she had never looked as beautiful as she did in that moment.

The maelstrom that was ocean and impact and force took them then. Their bodies disappeared into the wall of water that moved over the land with a force unseen in millions of years. In the hills beyond, forests fell, buildings exploded, and bridges disintegrated. All up and down the coastline, the scene repeated in varying degrees. Armageddon did not stop. It did not hiccup, nor pause. It claimed their lives without debate or question or compromise and rolled over a ravaged land, implacable and undefeated.

It did not stop until it reached the Rockies.

The Drowning Man

Quentin Lee didn't want to die.

When the glow in the sky had lit up the night with an eerie glow, and the air felt shot full of electricity, he knew it was time. Time to die. Along with countless others.

He had survived the initial chaos of the ESH virus. Sheer luck, really. He emerged from a months-long trek along the Appalachian Trail to find a world transformed. His buddy Max and an older couple from Des Moines had been his companions as they walked to Mirepoix, an Unaffected Persons encampment. Ill-fated, unfortunately, and that had been bad luck for Max.

Quentin had been one of a handful to walk away with his life, thanks to his AB negative blood.

He had even survived a stint fighting wildfires on the West Coast before they gave up and let the West burn to the ground. The smoke from those fires had tinged the Midwest sunsets with brilliant reds and oranges for months afterward.

But he wouldn't survive Azrael. No way, no how.

The impact projections had changed, fluctuated, nearly up to the last day. No one was completely sure how the smaller chunks of the massive asteroid would behave once they hit the atmosphere. Altitude and inclination, atmospheric conditions, speed - Quentin had lost track of all the different factors. It hadn't really mattered, anyway. His luck, if you could call it that, had run out.

He had lost out on the lottery, the first reading of the names, that Chairwoman Chen had announced. There had been more lotteries, more chances, but he wasn't well placed. He wasn't rich; he had no connections, no family, no pull. His education, a high school diploma and a smattering of lackluster college classes, had given him no opportunities. It was too late to study to be an engineer, or an artist, or a doctor. No time, and no one left to teach him the skills necessary to survive in the world to come. He didn't even have a place of refuge. He had seen the crowds, the wild-eyed people who jockeyed for position to board the flitters to the mountains in the west. It wasn't for sure he would have been any better off there. People individually can be dangerous enough, but in groups? The panic can overtake a person, make them a mindless beast, and he couldn't see how being stuck in a mass of desperate people vying over dwindling resources at the end of the world would be in anyone's best interest.

The politicians, those who had been rich before the virus destroyed the world, or those who had become rich in the great dying, well, they had a chance. But Quentin? And millions of others? Not a chance. No way.

Quentin could see the color changing to the south. Here, in the middle of nowhere, a nearby ancient brick grain silo had held for upwards of two hundred years or more. His vantage point was an ancient cell phone tower, the only one that graced the low, rolling hill above the dilapidated farmhouse to the east. He was higher, though, higher than he had ever been. Every step had been a fight against his instincts, ones that told him to stop, go no further, for man has no place at these great heights. No wings, neither feathers nor a bat's delicate membranes to break his fall should he slip. He hadn't thought of safety equipment. Of carabiner clips or harnesses. He'd just wanted to see the water when it came. He imagined it would hit with such force, such violence, that this solid structure would fold up like paper origami and it would sweep away him and it in the dark, black rush.

Above, the sky contained a few stars, but also great streaks of light. The thousands of meteors slid across the sky in a dazzling array of light and fire and, ultimately, destruction. Azrael was here, come to claim the last pitiful unfortunate. As far as he could see, the rolling hills and fallow farmland met low trees, and beyond, far beyond, a darkness rose. How far could the waters from the Caribbean come? And how tall would the waves be when they arrived? *Twenty-four years, two months, one week, eight, no, nine days.* He couldn't help thinking. *If I got a headstone, one of those old-fashioned ones, that's what it would read.*

They had tried to stop it; the Chairwoman had explained to the world. They had done their best to fracture it, make it smaller, less deadly. *Fourteen kilometers in diameter. No matter how much you chunk that up, it is like putting your finger on a crack in a dam. You might stop a few drops, but the rest?*

Whatever they tried, and they'd tried more than once, it hadn't been enough. Perhaps if the world's population had not been decimated to the tiniest fraction of what it was before the ESH virus. With all of those lost, there likely had been more than a few brilliant minds who might have solved the problem in time. There was simply no one left to stop the end of the world.

Quentin felt the wind pick up. It buffeted him, threatening to knock him from his perch long before the tsunami rushed over the land. He wrapped his arms around a strut, his legs folding like a yogi, his butt resting on a metal ledge that jutted out over nothingness.

"Impact point one - a ten kilometer chunk. Goodbye Hawaii, West coast, and Asia coastline." The wind increased, clawing at his words, but he could still hear them, just barely.

"Impact point two - a two kilometer chunk, hits the Alps. Impact point three, a one point two kilometer chunk in the Strait of Gibraltar and resulting mega-tsunami, gets the East Coast and most of Central and Latin America." He continued to recite from memory. Easier to think of this, than of his friends lost to the ESH virus, the panic of the world falling apart, and suicide.

"Impact point four, nine-tenths of a kilometer wide chunk that nails Cuba and sends another tsunami rocketing towards little ole me and a half kilometer chunk that will chomp Greenland." He continued, eyes fixed on the south. "And about fifty thousand errant pieces that will pepper our world with a critical case of acne."

The scientists had explained, in excruciating detail, the chaos that would follow. It wasn't the tsunamis and impact zones they had to worry about as much as what would come next. Nuclear winter. Years upon years of the sun being obscured by the ejecta forced into the atmosphere. A new ice age. No power or heat. No crops could be grown. Nor would solar arrays would work. And the best estimates were a minimum of eight years, possibly as long as eleven years, until the weather patterns recovered and the atmosphere cleared enough for food to be grown. There simply weren't enough food stores for fourteen million people to survive for that long. Only the enclaves, those vast underground structures, caves, and more, had any chance. And they were limited in space and scope. There was also the genuine chance that even the enclaves would not survive. If one of the smaller chunks of Azrael fell to Earth at just the right angle and wrong location, an entire enclave could be lost.

Clouds had formed. Roiling, dark, ominous. Or was it water? Quentin squinted. Try as he might, he could not tell. Here, hundreds of miles inland, a part of him dismissed it all. He'd be fine. Maybe the scientists and astronomers and all the rest were full of shit. Maybe they had calculated wrong. Perhaps the biggest piece, the one that they had predicted would hit the Hawaiian islands, would just slip into the oceans. Create an enormous wave, sure, but really, this world had seen worse, hadn't it? The other part of him practically gibbered in fear. The wrath of God, finally tired of the machinations of man, had tossed a rock bigger than their largest city to kill every squirming, upright monkey on Earth. No more global warming, climate change, war, pestilence. All gone, wiped clean from the land, finished now and forever.

It was water, not clouds. He could see it now. He stared, the gale-force winds trying to tear him from his perch, as it thundered toward him, a maelstrom of water and so much more.

As the force of it blasted under and past the cell tower, he felt more than he heard the structure groan, rivets popping, metal bending, snapping, as what was in the water itself rushed past. One moment he was a hundred feet up, the next, he could feel his body falling down toward the torrent. Swept up, submerged, his body twisting in agony and desperation.

This is how I die, Quentin thought, his last conscious thought as something slammed into him from behind, wrenching him from the dying world, his body rag-doll limp as the wave continued on.

This Is Going to Hurt

Quentin was pretty sure he wasn't dead.

Surely, being dead wouldn't hurt this damned much.

Somewhere away, he could hear water. A downpour. A dim light flooded to overwhelming brilliance as he cracked his eyes open. Blurred outlines, at least two, maybe three, people were around him. He opened his mouth to speak, but nothing came out. Nothing understandable, not even to his own ears. A groan, perhaps? Although it sounded more like a dog's whine.

The nearest blurred image resolved slightly as his eyes adjusted to the light. A fire crackled nearby. He could smell the wood smoke, hear the crackle and spit. The woman's face hung above him, blond hair heavily threaded with gray, cropped short, a gentle, compassionate face. She smiled at him.

"Hey there. Welcome back. I'm Ollie, by the way."

Quentin forced his mouth to work. "Not... dead?"

Her smile grew wider. "You look pretty alive to me. Can you tell me your name? Your age? What the date is today?"

Quentin winced as he pulled in enough air to answer her questions. His ribs were in agony. "Quentin. Quentin Lee. I'm..." A wet, hacking cough tore through him, sending sharp agony through his chest. "Uh, I'm twenty-four. And," he coughed again, foam burbling from his mouth and a chunk of something he had to turn and spit out. Wood, it had tasted like wood and blood. He blinked, trying to remember the date. Where he was. What could have happened to him? It was a blank. "Where am I?"

Ollie's hands passed over his left arm and a ragged half-scream tore from his lips. He would have screamed louder, but it hurt too much to breathe.

"Hurts, I know. I am sorry about that." She nodded to someone else close by. "Lindsay, hold the light right here for me, please." She gave Quentin a piercing stare. "Quentin, you are in a cave. The floodwaters have subsided, but there isn't much to see out there. The impacts have resulted in a large storm that looks as if it will be with us for a while. We are safe here for now. I need to set your left arm and bind your ribs if possible. And I am sorry, Quentin, but this is going to hurt."

Quentin opened his mouth to tell her it already hurt. A lot. But he couldn't really make the words work. Breathing was too hard. Moving was out of the question. He saw Ollie nod to the woman hovering, holding the light.

"That's the right angle, Lindsay. Hold it steady." Ollie moved over, away from him, and gave him a compassionate half-smile that spoke of regret. She pulled on his arm, decisively, and with a strength and speed, he found surprising from such a petite frame.

Quentin hadn't thought it possible to scream again. In fact, when it issued from his throat, it startled him, sure it was from someone else. Thankfully, the scream faded as quickly as his consciousness.

The Dark of Day

When Quentin next roused, his eyes were mere slits. Everything was dark, and what wasn't was blurred and hard to see. Around him were masses of clothes, stacks of food, and the ever-present fire crackled and spit. He couldn't hear the rain. Instead, there was a chill in the air. He could sense movement, others walking back and forth, work being done.

I should help somehow.

He tried lifting his head. "Rest Quentin," Ollie's voice reassured him, "You have plenty of healing to do."

"Can't... see... well."

"There was swelling from your being battered about in the water. You are a splendid array of black and blue bruises right now." She clucked sympathetically. "The best thing you can do is rest and try to drink some water if you are up to it." He could hear her rummaging around. "I have a straw here somewhere."

Some distance away, he could hear others talking in low voices. "Wrap it here and here. We can use it to block the incoming wind and snow."

Snow? In summer?

Ollie's face appeared above him, a straw in her hand. "Here, drink this. It has electrolytes and a bit of Nocdon crushed up. You need it. It will help with the pain."

He felt the straw at his lips and realized then just how thirsty he was. His mouth felt as if he filled it with grit and bitterness. He sucked at the straw, rewarded with a burst of sweet water, the tang of the electrolytes invigorating. When he reached the granulated Nocdon, there was a rush of bitter, but he swallowed anyway, desperate for some relief from the stabbing pain in every breath. He shifted then, and a rush of agony blasted through him.

Is it possible to hurt in places I never knew existed until now?

He realized he was half-naked, wrapped in shredded clothing, bandages and splints, and a thick, warm quilt.

Ollie, anticipating his question, shrugged and smiled. "The tsunami did its best to flay you alive. You got off better than most, you still have your pants. The rest, well, we had to cut off to get to your wounds and bind your chest. There's a nearby town, wiped out by ESH, but you never know. A group of four headed over to see if they can find anything to salvage earlier. Let's cross our fingers and hope they find something, including clothes."

"Where... are... we?" Every word was so damned hard. Just three of them and he felt as if he had run a marathon.

Ollie settled onto a blanket next to him and sighed. "I believe we are in the same cave that sheltered Jessica Farnsworth, a famous writer who lived through The Collapse and survived here, in this very cave, over a winter. You may have read it in school. It was called *Song of Survival.*"

Quentin remembered it. It had been required reading. The youngest of three children, his half siblings, had been ten and twelve years older. Deck, his older brother, had come home from school one day with a signed copy.

Her last book tour before she passed away a year later.

Another voice, younger, female, spoke from a few feet off. "I remember her describing that winter in the cave. Their preparations for it. How David bagged a deer before the first snowfall. With a bow and arrow, no less."

Quentin had loved the book. He'd snuck it out of Deck's under the bed box and read it cover to cover, long before the time came round to read it in school. But then again, he had loved stories of survival from an early age.

How many times did I read that antique book of mom's, Hatchet? *Five times? Ten?*

His mind wandered away from his discomfort, his pain, the hard stone floor he could feel underneath the rude pallet he lay on. It felt as if his thoughts were blurring now to match his eyesight. He felt Ollie's hand on his forehead. She murmured something, but he was already slipping away, the dark of day and the Nocdon pulling him back under, into the abyss of sleep.

A Key to Survival

It was four days before the scavenging team returned. By then, Quentin could sit up and move around. His left arm ached, and he longed for more Nocdon. Ollie had already told him how important it was to conserve it and it wasn't as if anyone would make anymore soon. He kept his aches to himself and tried to be thankful. They had fished him out of the floodwaters, half-dead, and patched him up. So far, he had done little but use up resources.

There isn't much I can *do one-handed and bandaged from head to toe.*

The swelling had receded enough for him to see again. He'd asked Lindsay for a mirror and stared at the battered, unrecognizable image in the small compact. Bruises danced across other bruises, cris-crossed with lacerations, cuts, and, in one case, a chunk of missing ear. The rough black stitches showed

Ollie had sewn it back into position as best she could. There was another divot of missing flesh on the back of his left arm, but he couldn't examine the full extent of that with only a hand mirror and dim firelight. He'd surveyed the damage and then handed the mirror back to Lindsay.

"You look like the loser in a bar fight. Bottom of the pile." The woman had told him. She pulled her stringy hair back into a ponytail. Lindsay looked as if she was in her mid-40s, and it had surprised Quentin to hear she was just a few years older than him. She had sighed at his look of surprise. "I was an addict. Got hooked on the Noc. Lost my kid." She had flashed a rare smile then. "He got a seat on a lifeship, though. He's snoozing on the Sana on Mars right now. At least I know he's okay, y'know? I got clean after I lost him, but it was too late to qualify. No room for reformed junkies on the lifeships."

There was a small thread of bitterness in her voice. Then she had shrugged and winked at Quentin. "We need to get you upright so you can help around here. Steer clear of the Noc and rest up and heal."

Ollie had fished Lindsay out of the waters too. Along with most of the other survivors. Most of the others had been in good shape, aside from bruises and lacerations, but two had died while Quentin was unconscious.

"Ollie did everything she could, but they were in awful shape. It was all I could do to help dig the graves. I have a hard time catching my breath since Impact. She thinks I got a cracked rib when Steve pulled me up into the boat."

There were nine survivors now that the scavenging team had returned. They had come in just as the darkness of night had sucked the last light out of their already dim world. Outside, the snow grew deeper and the guttural growl of a snowmobile had heralded their arrival.

A damned gas engine. Now if that isn't a rare thing.

Gas engines had been legislated out of existence shortly before The Collapse. Dwindling oil reserves had led to advances in electric cars. If the scavenging team were driving gas-powered anything, they had to be antiques.

"Christ, it is colder than a witch's tit out there." One man shivered after they had brought large bundles of supplies inside and they had placed the woven walls together to close off the narrow opening at the front of the cave. The man was tall, broad-shouldered, and Quentin could see the healing lacerations on the man's face among a smattering of freckles as he tore at his cold, damp clothes and clumped over to the fire. The man spared him a glance. His red hair was growing out of its buzz cut and looking rather shaggy.

"Still alive? Good on you, mate." His voice held a distinct Aussie twang and his eyes were a brilliant green hue. "Figured they destined you for the dirt like the other two."

Quentin blinked, unsure of what to say in response.

The bigger man reached out and clapped him on the shoulder. "Well, good to meet you. I'm Steve Dearborn, by the way."

"Quentin." He said it without groaning in pain from the man's hand on his shoulder. His body remained a mass of healing wounds and bruises, and Steve Dearborn had clapped his meaty hand directly over a healing contusion. "Quentin Lee."

Lindsay thrust a cup of steaming tea in Steve's hands. "Here, drink that."

Steve groaned in relief, turning away from Quentin and sinking into an open spot close to the fire. "Ah, Christ, I think I'll just hang on to the little fucker and defrost my digits."

The other three followed suit, shedding their damp outerwear, accepting steaming cups of tea, and hunkering down in front of the fire. The waves of chill air rolled off of them. No one said much as they warmed and slowly sipped the tea.

The rest of the group gathered. Their projects abandoned for the moment, eyes on the returning group, hopeful of good news. Finally, Steve spoke.

"First off, the town is in ruins. Not a single wall stands. It was in a valley, low enough to get hit hard by the floodwaters. So we're better off here than there. Better with a cave surrounding us than an open sky. We got three large bags of food. Canned goods mainly, some clothes, heavy winter gear, a handful of medicines for you to go through, Ollie. I told Addie to just clear the shelves and toss it all in a bag for you to look through. A blanket or two." He slurped the last of the tea and nodded at Lindsay's offer for more, holding his cup out for her to fill it, using a small pot as a ladle. "But the genuine gold came in while we were poking around there." He dug into his back pocket and pulled out his tablet. "Not all the cell towers are gone. The ones up on the hills, they're still transmitting. I'm guessing the government retrofitted them with enough battery power to keep going for a while. Long enough to send out the location of a redoubt within range."

"A re-what?" Quentin asked, frowning.

"A redoubt. It's a place of retreat of sorts." Steve waved his hands about, his cup sloshing slightly, droplets of tea splashing onto the floor of the cave.

"The fuckers couldn't have told us about it *before* the damned end of the world?" Lindsay asked, incredulous.

"Survival of the fittest." Ollie said quietly, her eyes on her own cup of tea. "Too many people, not enough shelter or supplies."

"So they wait until we're mostly dead and then tell the walking wounded 'go here.' Is that it?" Lindsay's voice rose in anger.

The others murmured in agreement. Ollie ignored them. "Exactly."

Quentin felt sick at the thought of it. He also wondered just how far it was and if it was physically possible for him to get there. *Can I hang on one-handed to the snowmobile? How far away is this place?*

"So how far is it?" He asked.

"One hundred twenty-five klicks, give or take another ten to fifteen for terrain and uncertain road conditions."

One hundred twenty-five klicks might as well be on the other side of the planet. There's no way I'm holding on for that long.

"Shit." One of the other muttered. "One hundred twenty-five klicks. In a blizzard. With only two snowmobiles and nine people. How are we gonna get everyone there?"

Ollie spoke again, softer than ever. "We aren't. We can't."

The voices rose. The panic rose along with it.

"Others will hear the broadcast."

"Can't just leave people to die."

"Need a team to go there and bring supplies back."

"Maybe relay? Stops along the way?"

"Are you stupid? We need to get there, and do it *now,* before someone else gets there and takes it all."

Quentin couldn't take his eyes off of Ollie. She knew something about this.

He raised his voice as loud as he could. His ribs were still in agony, his bruises fading from blacks and blues to greens and yellows, but only one laceration remained infected. A damned miracle considering the muck his body encountered in the floodwaters. He made himself heard.

"I'd like for you all to let Ollie speak, please." Ollie shot him a guilt-riddled look, one that told him his instincts were right. "Ollie? What do you know about this?"

The older woman set down her cup and looked at the group huddled around the fire. She took in a deep breath and stood up, wringing her hands.

"My, um, I guess you could call him my son-in-law. He was in the military. He heard of the plan for the redoubts. When I told him I was staying here, on the surface, instead of going in the lifeship, he told me about them. The plan for them." Ollie paced, moving away from the campfire, tidying, smoothing, her fingers nervously working. "It would never have been enough for everyone. The government knew it, the military too. After everything we had been through, after so much death... here they were, looking at the death of the world. Ten years. The predictive models say it will be ten years before the skies clear and the world recovers enough to be livable again. There wasn't a way to produce enough food and supplies for everyone, but they wanted to do something. The redoubts were the answer. Food stores, shelter, clothing, medicine, and more. The locations of them set to broadcast starting the day after Impact."

"It's been six, almost seven days now." The woman, Addie, interrupted. "Six days of that damned broadcast going off."

"How many redoubts are there, Ollie?"

Ollie stopped pacing. Shrugged. "I do not know."

"So we have a place of sanctuary, one over a hundred klicks away. With a cell tower blasting its location to anyone with range. And unknown numbers of people heading for the redoubt with six days' advance knowledge over us. Have I got that right?" Steve said, sarcasm dripping in his words.

Ollie flashed him a look and nodded.

"Well, we're fucked." Lindsay said. She cast a glance over at Ollie. "Sorry, Ollie."

Ollie sat back down, looking dejected. "No need to apologize, Lindsay. I agree with you."

"So what now?" Quentin asked.

"I rest up and head back out tomorrow." Steve answered heavily. "Who's coming with me?"

Lindsay raised her hand. "I'll go. If I stay here waiting, I think I'll lose my mind."

Two others, a man and a woman, raised their hands as well.

"All right," Steve said, "best get some rest. We head out tomorrow at first light." He gulped the last of his tea, walked over to an area where the cots were arranged and lay down, pulling a ragged blanket over his broad shoulders and putting his back to the fire.

White Out Conditions

The next morning, the inhabitants of the cave were awake with the dawn. It was a slight improvement overnight, but the snow was heavier than ever, creating whiteout conditions outside of the shelter of the cave. They lashed the cans of fuel to the vehicles, along with neatly folded tarpaulins that would serve as tents. The aged, vintage snowmobiles could clock up to thirty klicks an hour. A mere snail's pace when compared to their modern counterparts, but the best they had in the circumstances. Steve seemed sure they would arrive at the redoubt the same day, but Ollie had cautioned him to prepare to be out overnight.

"There's nothing worse than being under-prepared. Those are white out conditions out there. Take the tarpaulins and use them as tents if you have to spend the night outside."

Steve hadn't argued and Quentin watched from his fireside perch as Lindsay and Steve were joined by Juniper and Malcolm. The two had been acting like a couple, but Malcolm had mentioned a day or two that before Impact, they had been strangers, just like the rest of the survivors. Fate had brought them together.

After the group left, and the snowmobiles engines had faded into the distance, their rough motors broadcasting every hill, every dip, until they moved too far away for him to hear anything past the occasional grumble of thunder, Quentin picked at an itchy, healing cut on his arm. He hated sitting here, day in and day out, doing nothing. He had said as much to Ollie, who had laughed and told him, "You aren't doing *nothing*, Quentin, you are *healing*, and that is taking all of your energy. Get it done, then you will help us better." She had checked over his bandages, the healing abrasions, and tsked with concern at the one that wasn't healing as fast as the others. "If this doesn't get better by tomorrow, let me know. Addie and I went through the meds, and they found a good supply of antibiotics in the remnants of the town pharmacy. We need to make them last, but that one cut isn't looking so good."

"It'll be fine." Quentin resisted the urge to pick at a section that was throbbing in time with his heartbeat. It didn't look good, true, but he had taken up enough resources sitting here, eating, and doing nothing. He suspected the older woman could read his mind later in the day when she asked for his help to stir a pot of soup at the fire.

The days ticked by. One, two, three, and four days. Outside, the wind howled, and the snow continued to fall. Around twice a day, a group of two or three of them would move the partitions aside and survey the horizon. There wasn't much to see past a growing landscape of white. The green of the land was now obscured. Anything green obliterated first by the filth of the floodwaters and later by the snow. The things found in the remnants of the flooding were ever-changing. The tsunami had taken everything from the impact point in Cuba, where it had likely annihilated the island in a firestorm, all the way through a swath of Louisiana, Arkansas, Mississippi, and up into Missouri and even Iowa. Quentin wondered if anything remained of New Athens, with its shining spires of white. The city that had risen on the Midwest plains out of the ruins of the ESH virus had been stunning. It had promised rebirth and hope. They had dashed those hopes before Azrael ever arrived. The laws the TUPG passed that limited women's reproductive rights and ripped apart families were unlike anything Quentin had ever heard of, except in the works of fiction.

He wasn't any great intellectual. He didn't have a higher education past the basic high school education. But Quentin had been an avid reader in high school, and especially when he walked the AT. Sure, those had been all audiobooks, but he had gone on a science fiction tear as he walked the Appalachian Trail, lost in the story. Max had been the same. They had listened to a library of turn-of-the-century fiction as they made their way from the wilds of Maine all the way south, to Georgia. Emerging from the trail to a world in chaos had been like something out of the stories they had listened to.

They had rented a flitter, tried to get back to California, only to be turned away at checkpoint after checkpoint, before finally ending up in Sanctuary, better known by the other refugees as Mirepoix, near the Texas and Mexico border.

And look how that ended. Max dead. Most everyone else is dead.

There had been no reason to go back to California. He had spent six and a half months on the AT next to the love of his life and still couldn't get the courage up to tell Max how he felt. Another month at Mirepoix and a sheer week of hell as the virus erupted and spread like wildfire through the population, devouring Max in its wake. Quentin had spent his last days as a teenager watching his only friend in the world die. His dad had gone when he was young, his mother apathetic. No siblings. No extended family.

The four years since had been little more than survival. Months in refugee camps, standing in line for showers, for meals. He had gotten used to standing in lines. It hadn't really bothered him when he didn't find his name on the lists for the lifeships or underground sanctuaries. It had just felt like another sign that he wasn't meant for this world. Would anyone really care if he left? He was no one. He had no special skills. Not even basic survival skills past camping and being able to fall asleep anywhere thanks to those months on the Appalachian Trail.

"What's that burning smell?" Addie asked, leaning in close.

"Shit!" He grabbed the wooden spoon, ignoring the spike of heat on his bare fingers. A clump of stew was now firmly stuck to the bottom of the pot.

He looked around, embarrassed, but only Addie had seemed to notice and her round, dark face looked amused, not upset.

"It's no big deal, Quentin."

But it was. The food they had found in the ruins of the town wouldn't last forever, and it wasn't as if they could grow more. There had been talk of another expedition, or even a hunting party, but with no weapons save knives, Quentin thought Dean and Tilden were likely full of hot air. They were stir crazy, with little or nothing to do here in the cave, and were pissed they hadn't fit on the snowmobiles with the others to find the redoubt. The two of them had spent most of yesterday talking loudly about how they had told Steve and the others it should be the men who went in case there were issues. Issues apparently meant violence, Addie had commented quietly to Quentin, something they felt the women incapable of handling.

"Chauvinism will never die." She had whispered mostly to herself.

Never mind that there was no way for them to fit two men on each of the snowmobiles and expect to bring a heavy load back as well. They each stood over 1.8 meters tall and weighed at least 100 kilos each, whereas the women were each sixty kilos soaking wet. It would likely have been best to have only two on the expedition. But if anything went wrong, if one of them were hurt, it would have been just one person left out there in the snow alone. Nine people's lives hung in the balance, and they reviewed every decision, argued and second-guessed them, as the days slowly slipped by.

Only One

On day nine, the choppy sound of a snowmobile engine sounded above the wind and blowing snow. With nothing else for miles around, the growl of the engine was clear as day, loud, then muted. As it made its way laboriously over each hill, the sound squelched each time it dipped down into a valley. It took so long to arrive that Quentin and the others were forced by their numb fingers and toes to return inside to the warmth of the campfire. Dean and Tilden stayed outside, swearing and stomping, as they waited for the snowmobile to make its way, sputtering and coughing, to the entrance of the cave.

One snowmobile. Not two. One person, not four, although two bodies wrapped in a tarpaulin, showed disaster. Quentin and the others rushed out, helping the lone returnee to their feet. They pulled the various packages and boxes inside. The bodies they left on the snowmobile for burial later. There was nothing that could be done for them now. They were past help, and certainly past caring.

Once inside, the group made stumbling, awkward progress to the fire. There, with the snowy, damp layers pulled back, Quentin could see that it was Lindsay. Ice coated her eyelashes. Her cheeks were ruddy red blooms of color in an otherwise pale face, her lips gray, almost bloodless. She had collapsed the moment she tried to stand and Tilden and Dean had carried her inside, slipping, sliding, and swearing in the snow.

Ollie took charge. Quentin watched as she honed in on Lindsay, talking to her, coaxing the woman back from her semi-conscious state. It was a miracle she had made it back as bad as she looked at the moment. Her hands and feet were pale white.

"Where is the other snowmobile, Lindsay? What happened to Steve and Malcolm? Where's Juniper?" Dean was hovering close, his bulk impeding Ollie as she tried to slide the damp, snow covered outerwear off of Lindsay. He planted his feet on the stone floor, ready to demand answers, ignoring Addie as she gently pulled on his arm.

"No, we need to know. The other snowmobile might be out there, full of supplies. We can't wait until she recovers or feels better. We need to know."

Lindsay just sat there, shivering, her entire body shaking uncontrollably. "D-d-dead, I think. Back near the redoubt." Her blue lips juddered the words out.

Ollie placed a hand on Dean's chest, a stern look on her face. "Back off, Dean. Unless you learned some nursing, or have a special knowledge of frostbite treatment I don't know about, then you need to back off."

Quentin saw a steely side of the older woman he hadn't known existed. She was willing to take on a man who had at least half a meter and over forty kilos on her.

Dean stopped, frowned, and then retreated, moving the partition outside to return to the snowmobile and retrieve the supplies that were lashed to it. He returned a few moments later in another swirl of snow and cold air, tugging at an enormous container labeled MRE. Tilden and Addie ran to help him drag the monstrosity in through the cave entrance and then replacing the partitions that held back the worst of the cold air and snow.

The food had dwindled to just a few days' worth, used judiciously. This, however, was a heartening improvement. As they dug down into the container, bringing the MREs over into the light by the fire, Quentin could see that they would be in good shape for a while. Weeks, possibly even months. In addition, Lindsay had returned with a rifle and ammunition, also manually rechargeable lights with a dial you turned. With the lights, they could explore the tunnels branching off of the cavern. With the rifles and ammo, they could hunt. There were deer in the region, wild turkey, and more.

Ollie was still working on Lindsay, now unclothed, her extremities being bathed gently in warmed water. This was likely to combat any frostbite, Quentin assumed. Her eyes were closed and her shaking had slackened. Now the tremors came intermittently, usually in response to stimuli. Dean looked as if he wanted to question her again, and took a step towards the semi-conscious woman. Before he could return to Lindsay, however, Tilden placed a beefy hand on Dean's shoulder and murmured in his ear. It seemed she had earned some respite from questioning with the tiny amount of information she had given. There was nothing to be gained by interrogating the woman right now.

Ollie sealed the deal by saying, "She needs rest. If you are damned and determined to find out what she knows, follow the tracks back. Otherwise, you will all need to wait for your answers. She's dehydrated, has frostnip, and is exhausted. And that's just what I can see on the surface." Her tone brooked no argument, and burly as they both were, neither Dean nor Tilden seemed ready to take Ollie on.

An entire day passed and Lindsay barely moved. She was a lump of blankets there near the fire, a silent mystery surrounding her. Quentin noticed that the other denizens of the cave all found excuses to walk close to where she was, likely as curious and concerned about what had happened as he was. No one bothered her, though. Ollie stayed close and was the only one who approached Lindsay.

Both Dean and Tilden had spent a large part of the day digging into the soil several yards outside of the cave. By the time they finished, Quentin had, at Ollie's request, scratched out another hash mark on the cave wall. There were two here he didn't remember, the days when he was semi-conscious, or sleeping thanks to the Noc after Ollie had set his arm. Another four from the days when he sat upright and the first team of four went scavenging in a local town. Nine more hash marks from the second expedition, and now he added another. Had it really been over two weeks since Impact? Apparently, it had.

He was moving around better now. His arm ached, but it wasn't bad enough to keep him awake at night as it had the first ten days. He'd made the mistake of brushing too close to the cave wall when visiting the latrine, a couple of days ago. The hard stone against his bound, injured arm had caused points of light and pain to flare in front of his eyes, and he had slammed into the far wall as if repulsed by a cattle prod. Healing was something that took time, something they had an ample share of as temperatures continued to drop and the snow fell. It was now a daily chore to clear a path out of the cave to the lake several hundred yards beyond. Addie, Dean and Tilden did that, as well as trying each day at fishing in the rapidly freezing lake. If they didn't clear it, the snow would block their egress entirely. The only positive was the fact that snow was insulating. The temperature inside of the cave had risen even as the temperatures outside continued to drop. This meant less need for firewood, and less of a shortage of cold-weather gear. The parkas were reserved for those who needed to make the trek outside.

Branching off from the main cavern was a warren of smaller passages. They had extensively mapped these over the years since they had turned the cave into a tourist attraction in the mid-2060s. This had followed the rise in popularity of Jess Farnsworth's book, *Song of Survival*. One passageway led to a sharp drop off. So sharp, in fact, that it was impassible without rappelling gear, lights, and more. The passageway narrowed to two waist-high boulders wide enough to slip through. Then the drop, which had to be at least fifty feet, was beyond that. And as nuts as it sounded, this was the perfect place for a latrine. It was a challenge at first, especially with one broken arm, but the others would walk to the boulders, turn around, drop their pants, grab hold of the rock, and release their bowels into the void below. It was a hell of a sight better than going out into the snow to do their business once one got over the stomach-clenching fear of falling.

God help us if we ever need to go down there for any reason. We'd be sliding down into a pile of shit!

The chances of that were unlikely. If the map was accurate, that drop off ended in a small cavern with no other outlet. The rest of the connecting passageways snaked off deep into the hillside, sometimes for half a mile or more. And because of the depth of the drop, the smells were far enough away as to be nonexistent.

The Bounty

Quentin had just returned from his morning constitutional when two things happened at once. Two bloodcurdling screams. One from Lindsay, who was suddenly sitting up, eyes wild, half-awake and obviously disoriented. The other scream was from Addie, who dashed from the passageway at the opposite side of the cavern, a look of terror on her face.

"What the hell?" Dean, having just come from shoveling duty outside, clumped towards first Lindsay and then turned away and headed for Addie. Whatever had Lindsay screaming, it was likely from her trip to the redoubt and back, but whatever Addie was screaming over, well, that had to be more imminent.

"Dead! Some dead guy! Back down, around the second curve!" Addie babbled, obviously rattled. The lantern swung wildly in her grip as she pointed into the dark passage.

Ollie reached for Lindsay; the younger woman's eyes as big as saucers. "Lindsay, honey, you're safe." She looked up, made eye contact with Quentin and angled her head towards the passageway, clearly telling him to go find out what Addie had seen.

Quentin crossed the cavern and caught up to Dean, who was already slipping the lantern out of Addie's hand. Addie fled, running back to light and warmth, looking pale and sick.

Quentin had to double time it to keep up with the bigger man as he marched into the tunnel. He needed to stay close. The light from the lantern extended only a few feet in each direction. After that, the inky blackness descended, sucking all the light out of the world. The passageway was long, and a moment or two passed until they reached the first curve. Dean headed toward the right, but Quentin grabbed the larger man's sleeve. "She said the second curve. It's further, on the left." He hadn't been down this passageway, but the map positioned at the entrance to it had shown the depth. They had already come at least fifty feet, possibly more, and the second curve was another seventy-five feet or more.

Dean stopped, lifted the lantern higher and stared into the darkness on the right. "You sure?"

"Yeah, straight ahead, another seventy-five feet, maybe more."

Dean picked up the pace, and Quentin did his best to keep up, stumbling any time he dropped out of range of the light. Dean didn't slow. The man acted like a damned bloodhound, single-minded and oblivious to anything but the task at hand. The smell hit them first. A sickly-sweet scent of decay that quickly intensified the closer they came.

A body lay crumpled along one wall. Something easily missed at first glance. It was wearing a uniform, the last name of Pierce embroidered on the front.

"A grunt. What the fuck was he doing here?" Dean set the lantern down, covered his mouth and nose, and leaned closer. The man's skin was leathery, dried.

Quentin wondered how long the body had been here. He glimpsed something large in the passageway beyond, just outside of the circle of light. His eyes strained, trying to figure out what it was. No luck. It remained a hulking thing in the dark, with no real clarity. That was the thing about caves, though. There was no light, so it didn't matter how long you waited for your eyes to adjust, they never really would. The only thing that helped was adding light to the equation. He reached over, grabbed the lantern, and walked past the corpse further into the passageway.

"Hey!" Brad growled in frustration as the light left him shrouded in darkness, with only the dead man for company. But he fell silent, his mouth gaping open at what Quentin had found.

An enormous stack of MREs. And not just one stack. No, there were more, lots more. Pallets of them. They occupied most of the width of the passageway and Quentin had to slide to the right side to get through. The pile kept on going further and further down. There had to be months of supplies here. Maybe even years if they were judicious about it. It wasn't the amount they might have found at the redoubt, but Quentin had to wonder if it perhaps had been part of the redoubt supplies that this man had instead brought here.

Not a bad idea, except you died hiding it here. And what good would it do you?

No good at all.

"Holy shit. Is that what I think it is?" Dean asked, his voice a whisper.

"Enough food to keep us alive for months? Yeah." Quentin answered, his voice a whisper as well.

No need to bellow. No need to disturb the dead.

He found the end of the supplies and edged his way back to the reeking corpse. By then, Dean had found another lantern, obviously the one belonging to the dead man, and cranked it until the light filled the passageway.

"No injuries, I can see. Maybe Ollie could tell us what happened to him." Dean said, rifling one-handed through the corpse's pockets, other hand held hard against his mouth and nose. Quentin felt his bile rise in response.

A wealth of food, medicine, and other supplies just waiting for them here. Quentin thought of the others - Juniper, Malcolm, Steve - all dead. They had gone to the redoubt to survive, and ended up paying with their lives. While here, there was the key to survival the entire time, if only any of them had thought to look for it.

It's not as simple as that. We had no lanterns, nothing to light the way in the darkness, and no way of knowing.

Part of him still felt guilty, though. Even more so as he calculated how much more meals not having to feed those three mouths would mean for the rest of them. Months of meals, perhaps.

Babies are Loud

The longest winter in recent human history ended, or at least a brief rest, some eight months later. The skies remained overcast, but the snow had stopped falling. Everywhere, water dripped. A creek had emerged, rushing past the opening of the cave, headed toward the lake beyond. It was enough of a respite that the baby's cries felt like a promise of something new. Rebirth, perhaps.

He was small, red, and angry. Quentin and the others gathered close now that the goriest part of it was done. Even Dean and Tilden, who both looked rather green at all the blood and fluids that accompanied the birth of another human. Here in this enclosed space there was also that animal smell, warm, primal. Lindsay held him close, her eyes shadowed with exhaustion. It hadn't been easy. Her labor had lasted for nearly two days. Ollie looked just as exhausted, not surprising since she had been by Lindsay's side, helping and supporting her the entire time.

The baby calmed as Addie gently wiped his face with a warm, wet cloth and the baby's head turned, rutting instinctively for the one and only thing of comfort he needed. A few moments of fumbling later and he was nursing contentedly, tiny mews not unlike a kitten issuing from the bundle of cloth.

"He's beautiful, Lindsay." Addie murmured, as she helped Ollie clean up the immediate area.

Lindsay's chin trembled briefly, tears pooling in her eyes. "He is."

Ollie sat down on the other side of Lindsay, tiredness etched into her face. "Have you thought of what to name him?"

Lindsay sat quietly, staring at the babe in her arms. Finally, she spoke. "Ethan. It means firm, enduring, strong, and long-lived. My grandfather's name was Ethan."

"It's a good name." Ollie said, and she smiled and leaned back to rest on a bundle of clothes and bedding. "Enduring, I like that. Endurance is a trait a person needs in this new world."

Quentin was silent. He was thankful Lindsay, and the baby, were all right. Over the months, he had grown closer to her, listened as she told him about her son Robert. She has shared her dreams for a future where she could greet him as he emerged from the lifeship. Even her childhood growing up on the bayou in a tiny Louisiana parish.

Whatever had happened to Lindsay at the redoubt, she had refused to speak of it. She had said only that they had killed Malcolm and Steve shortly after they had all arrived there and that she and Juniper had got away, load up supplies, the bodies already there on the sled, and that something had happened to Juniper as they were leaving.

The baby's hair was jet black, a full head of tight curls. His skin, now that the shock of birth had faded, was a deep olive hue. Lindsay's skin was as pale as milk. Blond hair. Steve's had been red, with pale, freckled skin. It didn't take a genius to put two and two together. The father of Lindsay's child hadn't been Steve.

It could have been some rando before Impact. It's possible.

The way she had cried and rocked back and forth. The nightmares. Waking up screaming nearly every night for months. Those had spoken of something far worse having happened. Worse than seeing the men and Juniper murdered in front of her. A week or more of it, by his guess.

Quentin watched as she kissed the baby's head and rocked back and forth. Part of him wondered if she would ever tell them what had happened there at the redoubt. Another part of him knew it was irrelevant to the here and now. They were alive, all six of them, seven now if they counted the baby. There were months and months of supplies now, supplemented by what they could hunt and fish. He listened to the steady drip of melting snow, the rush of the creek beyond the cave entrance, and the tiny snuffling kitten-like mews of the infant at Lindsay's breast.

Eight and a half months ago, he'd been clinging to a cell tower watching death approach. It had washed over him and tossed him aside. Death had rejected him. Since then, he and the other survivors had worked together, become friends, and buoyed each other's spirits through the long winter. Working together toward a common goal, that of survival.

Quentin Lee didn't want to die. Not yet. And right now? Being here, alive, was all that really mattered.

Casa Oceano

01.11.2109
Mediterranean Sea

It was the terrible groan, movement, and a general shifting that woke Lexi from her sleep.

They had fought last night, her wife, Tamara, and her. Despite this, in their sleep, they had migrated toward one another, closing any gap caused by their bitter words, healing the rift as their bodies drifted together. Tamara snuggled close against her. Her breaths tickled Lexi's ear. It had been this way since they first met. Their touches might no longer be electrical, or their lovemaking new and innovative, but their bodies sought the comfort and reassurance of the other in sleep.

It was dark, pitch black. The bedroom had portholes in it, just as every level and outer ring of their ocean home did. On the eighth level from the surface, over one hundred feet beneath the surface of the ocean, there was no natural light. At precisely five in the morning, the perimeter lights would turn on, and after that, the interior lights as well. Lexi Santfeli ran a tight ship, and except for a skeleton crew at night, they expected every resident of the Casa Oceano ocean spiral to be up and at their posts by seven.

"What the hell was that?" Tamara croaked. A nasty head cold had been making the rounds in the past week. That had been the source of their argument. Lexi had insisted that Tamara rest, and her lover, miserable and sick, had accused her of favoritism.

"You would never let the refugees get away with that excuse." She had accused, blowing her nose into a handkerchief. Supplies were limited on board. And five years in since Azrael had descended upon their world, paper products were gone. No more toilet paper, no more tissues.

Tamara wasn't wrong. Since that first tumultuous day, with only a few exceptions, Lexi had regretted taking on the refugees. They weren't researchers or scientists, and sometimes, they didn't have any usable skills. It had made life difficult and reminded Lexi of why she lived on the ocean spiral in the first place. She didn't particularly *like* people.

A shaking and screams followed the groan and shifting. Sound carried in the spiral. Despite their population being half of what they built Casa Oceano to handle, the engineers apparently had not anticipated how loud other humans could be. Or perhaps they hadn't cared. It mattered not. What did matter was that when a discussion got heated, your immediate neighbors could hear just about every syllable. Lexi, an incredibly private person, hated it. Tamara, when angry, grew loud while Lexi spoke quieter. She was sure the entire eighth level knew their business, and Tamara's opinion of her. Likely the seventh and ninth levels as well.

"Thetis, lights!" The AI computer on board Casa Oceano obeyed instantly. The lights overhead brightened to full day levels.

"There has been a disturbance on Level 35," Thetis spoke, his synthetic voice calm.

"Yeah, no shit." Tamara croaked, coughing as she pulled on her clothes.

"Where do you think you are going?" Lexi asked, frowning at her lover. "You need to stay in bed."

Tamara glared at her, likely remembering she was still angry at Lexi. She opened her mouth, only to be interrupted by a shaking, the flickering of lights, and their abrupt departure, plunging the room back into blackness.

"Thetis, lights!" The computer didn't respond, but the ambient sounds around them certainly did. Voices filled with fear, screams, and again, the feeling of movement. If they had been on one of the fishing vessels, or even the tiny submarine, Lexi could understand it. But they weren't. They were on an ocean spiral, one of a handful of underwater research stations built before the onset of the ESH virus and the asteroid that had plunged the Earth into a new ice age. Above them, the sea temps had plunged by nearly fifteen degrees and during the winter months, ice floes were common. Below the waterline, though, the spiral held steady, anchored to the sea floor by massive columns of steelcrete, which promised to last longer than humanity would at the rate it had been going. So what was causing the movement?

Her radio squawked then. Thank God for the radios. Battery powered, waterproof. The lights might be off, but the radios still worked. "Mayor, we got a problem down near the substation." It sounded like Olanti, which surprised Lexi. *Isn't he on the day shift?* Whether or not he was on the day shift appeared irrelevant now. They seated the substation and the source of their power directly over a geothermal vent. It had provided Casa Oceano with a steady source of power for over seven years, but something had definitely affected it. There had never been a power outage, not even when Azrael had impacted Earth.

"On my way!" Lexi radioed back. The radio continued to squawk as other levels reported in.

"Level 11, reporting in, we are without power."

"Level 18, same here."

"Level 5, ditto."

She turned it down until the radio became a murmur at her hip and, flashlight in hand, slipped from their tiny apartment and toward the center ramp. The elevator, which ran down the enormous middle shaft, some thirty-five stories in depth, was offline, but the ramp that wrapped around it was mostly clear. Occasionally, as she passed one of the residency levels, there were other people holding flashlights or the waterproof, deep-pressure lamps used in underwater expeditions. Lexi nodded at her fellow scientists and ignored the others. She didn't have time for pleasantries. The title of mayor had been honorary. She was the senior scientist on staff the day that Azrael fell to Earth. Olanti had called her mayor as a joke, and it had quickly spread. Now everyone called her mayor, and there had even been calls in the beginning to hold elections. Something quickly dispelled once she clarified that all politics aside, the refugees were not citizens of Casa Oceano and were here at the grace of others. It had caused plenty of grumbles, but the refugees, although they outnumbered the researchers and scientists who had been on the spiral already, did not object. They didn't know how to run the complex machinery, and most of them had lived on the mainland, without so much as experience in fishing to their credit. There were regular waves of discontent, but life here was better than out there. They were safe; they had enough food, and all the inhabitants of Casa Oceano, whether or not they belonged there, were invested in keeping the ocean spiral a sanctuary for all.

Lexi's strides were long, ground-eating, and the levels kept increasing the further down she walked. She felt her ears pop as well, close to Level 20. Casa

Oceano was in a relatively shallow section of the Mediterranean Sea, but the spiral city progressed all the way to the bottom of the sea floor, resting on the massive piers of steelcrete that anchored deep under the ocean floor. For it to shake like this meant that either there was a tectonic shifting of the continental plates or something was hitting the piers. The engineers who had designed the ocean spiral had planned for potential tectonic activity in the region and placed the spiral close to Cyrenaica, the eastern region of Libya. Less than a mile away from the mainland, Casa Oceano was relatively unaffected by the subduction zones of the Aegean Sea and African plates. Occasional tremors happened, but nothing like this.

Olanti was waiting for her at the bottom. He had been there long enough to set up several lanterns, and the room clearly illuminated. "It isn't seismic." He said in greeting. Lexi appreciated his direct words. Too many others dithered about and didn't get straight to the topic at hand.

"Okay, what is it then?"

Olanti grinned. A rare sight these days, as preoccupied as he had become with the daily survival needs of the spiral's occupants. "We have a whale fall. A big one. I think it's a blue whale. I'll know more when we can get out there."

Lexi's mouth fell open. "A blue whale *here* in the Mediterranean?" Her excitement rose. The researcher in her temporarily forgetting the cares of the past few years, or their current power failure. She wanted to study it, examine it if possible. They rarely found blue whales in the Mediterranean. This creature's presence here, its death, was an unusual find.

Olanti nodded and then grimaced. "Unfortunately, it has fallen in just the wrong place. It hit a pier first, which isn't an issue, but the tail landed against the substation, and I think the connection from the substation to the spiral is damaged, thanks to the weight of the beast."

Lexi's mind spun at the thought of it. A whale fall, *here*, of all places. It felt like both luck and tragedy. Blue whales could weigh up to 199 tons and measure nearly thirty meters. They could watch the creature be consumed by all manner of ocean life and document it all. *If* they could get the power back on.

"We will need to move it or disarticulate that section of it." Lexi replied, then winced at the thought of cutting into the majestic creature. No matter that the denizens of the deep would feast on its flesh, the thought of having to maim the corpse of the whale, cut its tail off, just so they could have their power restored, seemed grotesque, wrong.

"Mm hm." Olanti stared out the viewing window into the darkness. The emergency lights served as dim points of reference, lighting the path to the substation, and what was resolving into a decent view of the massive cetacean corpse now gracing the ocean floor. "You and me, Mayor?"

Lexi smiled then. How long had it been since either of them had the excuse of going out in one of the pressure suits and scouting about? Limited oxygen tanks, time, and energy restricted those expeditions. A thousand other activities kept them busy daily, and venturing out into the ocean was rarer than it should have been. "Sounds like a date."

Less than twenty minutes later, they were suiting up, a team of their colleagues surrounding them, Tamara in the far corner, hacking and coughing. Word had spread quickly, and they actually had very little time before there would be significant problems. Air quality at the top of that list. The ventilation systems depended on power to be fully efficient. Without electricity, the air in the lower levels would see an eventual rise in carbon dioxide levels, making it difficult, if not impossible, to continue working down here. And then there was the practical side of things. Eighty-two souls depended on the lights, the power, the heat, to live comfortably. A part of her was thrilled. Finally, an excursion into the world she had spent her life studying. The dark waters of the Mediterranean held so much life and mystery within them. The world above might have fallen apart, thanks to the ESH virus and the destructive might of Azrael, but the waters below told a different tale. No matter what happened above, the creatures in the sea would survive. Not all of them, but far more than those on land.

Suits had improved significantly in the past four decades as science had focused on the mysteries of the Earth's oceans. Thanks to breakthroughs in plastic polymers that could blend with steel, engineers had created pliable, yet strong suits capable of maintaining pressure at ever-increasing depths, while the slim packs on the backs of the suits allowed them to breathe, and speak. Dexterity in the fingers had increased, and Casa Oceano's suits were outfitted with small motorized jets that could propel them longer distances in the water if they should need it. Lexi loved these excursions. After five years of living on the spiral while the world above froze in its mini ice age, she had had fewer and fewer opportunities to slide into the suit and return to the underwater world she had pledged her life to study. Survival, however, had become far more important.

The passage from the moon pool, a pressurized, open-air pool set in the bottom of Casa Oceano, had been dark, so unlike a regular excursion into the sea. Without the bright surround of lights, it felt spooky, especially as something large passed by her and Olanti, felt more than seen, nothing more than an enormous shadow that seemed to dim the lanterns as they headed away from Casa Oceano towards the gigantic corpse.

Up close, the blue whale was even more immense. A female, no less, the larger of the species. From one end to the other, she was taller than a six story building. All Lexi wanted to do was run her hands along the body of the creature, learn its secrets. What had the poor girl gone through up there? Had she wondered at a world gone mad? The severe weather and a drastic reduction in ocean temps. How hard had it been for her to survive? Lexi wanted to examine the contents of the whale's stomach and look for clues. Had her diet changed in the past five years? How old was she when she died? The questions swirled through Lexi's brain. Blue whales can live up to one hundred years, sometimes a decade longer than that. The world that this whale could have seen, and experienced, in her lifetime, the changes on land and in the sea.

The cetacean was a time capsule. She had existed long before the ESH virus burned through 99.6% of the world's population, before the Calypso had left their solar system, possibly before the Mars and Moon colonies were founded. It was possible she had been here since before The Collapse.

"God, they brutalized her." Olanti's voice interrupted Lexi's daydreams. She looked at where he was pointing. Deep gashes, some a foot or more in depth, cris-crossed one flank.

"Anti-mortem? Or post-mortem?" Lexi asked as they drew close.

"Hard to tell. And you know she had to have been up there on the surface for a few days before the gasses expelled and she sank."

There were plenty of bite marks littering the corpse. Above them, in the water above, movement. Something large.

"Heads up, Olanti. We have company." Lexi pointed as first one, then another large body moved past. Great whites, at least two, were gliding through the gloom. Something else, too.

"We got a sleeper shark, maybe two."

Lexi aimed her light and peered into the gloom. "Make that four sleepers and at least three great whites." Around them, the sea floor was alive with activity, most of it seemed to trip along toward the corpse. The dinner bell had been rung, and pretty soon, they would have a wide range of sea life feasting on the massive whale. It would not, however, solve their problem soon enough. The whale's tail lay canted up at an angle on one end, one weathered and ragged edge covering the edge of the substation closest to their ocean spiral home. Lexi could see the thick black cable that led between the ocean spiral and the geothermic substation buried beneath the tail. Left alone, the incoming sea life would cover the corpse, feasting off of it for months, even years, until not even the bones would remain. This was, however, a long process. And Casa Oceano's inhabitants didn't have months to wait, they had mere hours until the lower levels would be impossible to breathe in.

"It doesn't look ripped loose, thank God, but we have to get the weight of that tail off of it." Olanti walked along the sea floor toward the tail end of the fallen beast, and his feet roiled the sediment into the water, clouds of it obscuring their view. More large shapes moved past, intimidatingly close. He bent down, his head and body momentarily disappearing into the swirling sediment, and Lexi could hear him grunt in exertion. "Shit, we're gonna need to cut through it. No other way around it."

"How?"

"I brought a knife."

Lexi laughed, then abruptly stopped when she realized Olanti was serious. "There's got to be another way."

"If you have one, I'm all ears. Meanwhile..." He brandished what looked like a cleaver from the kitchen on Level Ten. "I'm gonna get to work."

Lexi racked her brain for some kind of underwater equivalent to a chainsaw, and could think of nothing. Olanti swung, the knife burying itself deep into the rotting, cetacean flesh.

Olanti beckoned her over. "Here, I brought one for you, too."

Lexi laughed at the absurdity of it all. "Of course you did." She took her position on the other side of the massive tail and swung the knife. The density of the water rendered her move useless, and she quickly learned to cut the flesh by pushing her entire body behind the blade, forcing it deeper into the tail. Behind, above, and all around her, sediment and sea life swirled. She could see octopi in varying sizes attaching themselves up and down the corpse. The great white and sleeper sharks passed by, closer and closer, and that was anxiety-inducing. Thankfully, the whale corpse had little blood left in it. This seemed to disappoint the great whites, even as it attracted more and more sleeper sharks. Sleeper sharks, while still carnivorous predators, had long been considered relatively non-aggressive by the scientific community. At least, that was Lexi's understanding. Whether the research was incorrect, or the circumstances of this new post-apocalyptic world changed so drastically, or even that they were arms deep in dead whale flesh, Lexi wasn't completely sure, but the sleeper sharks seemed to have other ideas. While not as large as great whites, at twenty feet and over 300 kilograms, they were nothing to sneeze at. Their teeth were scary as hell, too. Their mouths were full of teeth designed to tear flesh from bone. Lexi felt them growing closer. Their initial curiosity at the strange land-creatures in their territory quickly waned in the face of hunger. And in the sea, everything was hungry all the time. The water was a kill or be killed home to some terrifying beasts.

As she hacked and stabbed her way into the tail, keenly aware of Olanti's presence just on the other side, she felt a hard push against her back. It knocked her off balance, caused her to slip and squirm, her hands trying desperately to catch anything substantial past the gruesome ravaged whale flesh in front of her. An enormous dark shape, larger than any of the others, sent her tumbling.

"Shit, that's a big one." Olanti said, and Lexi thought she could detect a note of fear in his voice.

She landed on her knees on the sea floor. The body of the whale rocked in place as the massive shape didn't so much as collide as it ripped an enormous divot from the whale's side.

"What the hell is that thing?"

"The biggest goddamn sleeper shark I've ever seen. It's gotta top seven meters and a thousand kilograms!" Olanti snapped back. "Why the fuck it's down here by the tail and not up at the head eating, I got no idea."

Lexi knew the answer, though. It was the two of them, moving, riling up the behemoth that had disappeared for now beyond the dim perimeter of their underwater lights. And it would continue to be bothered by their presence until they left it to its prize. She felt more than saw the impact of one shark against another. The larger one was eking out its territory, claiming its prize, and she was becoming increasingly convinced that it would turn its sights on them next. She stabbed at the connective tissue harder, desperate to get the tail cut and the pressure off of the line from the substation. She prayed that was all that it was. Just a few more inches closer to Olanti, just a few more hacks of her knife, and...

The impact of the shark into Olanti sent up a whirling dervish of sediment, obscuring everything. It also knocked the hacked tail sideways, and it ripped along the same lines Lexi had been cutting. The flesh weakened thanks to her efforts. She tumbled away, landing on the sea floor, the lights on her suit cockeyed and blinking erratically. Seconds later, the sediment was billowing up again, but further away, as the shark ripped and tore into the belly of the dead whale. But Lexi wasn't looking in that direction. Instead, she was staring at the body of her friend as it drifted with the water and the surrounding creatures. Loose. Limp. Headlamp gone. Lexi blinked. It didn't make sense. It had only been a few seconds. A few inhalations in and out. A handful of heartbeats.

"Olanti? Olanti!"

The lights aboard the ocean spiral blinked into existence, lighting up the ocean floor, and painting a far clearer, yet grim, picture of what had happened in those few precious seconds. Olanti, still in his suit, the clear protective bubble that should have been around his head was gone, ripped from its fastenings. It bobbed in the water a short distance away. How it had happened, and with such speed, Lexi still could not understand. But she understood death. She had watched it slide over her father, rip his soul from his body some fifteen years before in a bleak hospital room. And her mother barely a year later, encased in her loneliness and grief. She saw it in his eyes. Fixed. Unblinking. His mouth open, his body limp. There was no coming back from what she saw.

"No! No! No!" Lexi screamed. Not Olanti. Not this way, not here, not after all that they had been through.

She could hear Tamara's croaking voice carry over the radio then. Before, during the power outage, only the suits were connected, but now, with the massive weight of the whale's tail off of the power supply, Casa Oceano was back online, and so were the long-range radios.

"Lexi, baby? What's happened?" Her lover's voice sounded panicked, cracking from illness and fear.

Lexi couldn't bear to respond. She could barely breathe. The pain of the loss, so sudden, so unjust, tore through her. She climbed to her feet, made her way toward Olanti, caressed his face with her hand.

They had grown up climbing the cliffs and exploring the ocean's surf together in Paleo Trikeri, a tiny fishing village in Greece at the entrance of the Pagasetic Gulf. He had dreamed of becoming an oceanographer long before she had ever considered a future beyond those carefree, barefoot summer days. His family hadn't had the funds, however, and it had taken him years, a stint in the Navy, and years of intermittent schooling before their paths had crossed again, fortuitously, on Casa Oceano. And now he was gone. In a heartbeat. It wasn't fair. He deserved so much more.

She was halfway back, Olanti's body gently bumping along the floor, her hand tight around the rim of his suit, when the others joined her and took over, bringing the body of their friend back to the ocean spiral. In through the moon pool, back through the lights. Back home.

Blanca was waiting, Elisabet by her side. Five years ago, she had jumped into the sea with her infant daughter, following her husband. Olanti hadn't been able to save her husband. The man had sunk like a stone under the sea. But he had fished Blanca and tiny Elisabet out, revived the tiny babe, and helped them into the spiral in the moments before Azrael took the rest of the world in fire, flood, and blood. It had taken time. Months, more than a year, as Olanti visited the two of them daily. Eventually, Lexi had watched as Olanti, a sworn bachelor, grew closer to Blanca and a father figure for little Elisabet. There had come the day when they had moved in together. Not out of necessity, nor duty. Out of *love*. Lexi thought of that now, nearly four years later, as she stared into Blanca's eyes.

"It happened so quick. He was, he was just... gone." Blanca's features blurred as Lexi's eyes filled with tears.

Not Olanti. Anyone else. Me. I'm no hero, not like Olanti. This world, this shell of a world. It isn't fair.

Blanca folded up, as if her backbone had been Olanti, and without him her will to stand had evaporated. Little Elisabet stared at her mother, mute in the face of such tragedy. A muttering moved through the crowd.

Olanti had been the bridge between them all. Lexi might have been Casa Oceano's designated mayor, but Olanti had been the go-between. He had met everyone one-on-one, cleared up misunderstandings, helped the refugees assimilate to life on the ocean spiral, and guided Lexi to understanding those under her rule better. Olanti had policed those in need of rules, and provided a listening ear to the most sensitive among them. He had been their heart and soul. And he was gone. In one fateful twist of a creature's tail. Lexi wanted to hate the dead whale, the sleeper shark, the asteroid, anything, everything, that had conspired to take her best friend away from her.

Elisabet stepped away from her mother, who lay inert on the floor of the room. She walked the few steps to Olanti's body and leaned down to cup his face, much the same as Lexi had there on the ocean floor. Her tiny hand caressed his beard. "Goodbye, Papa."

Seven Months Later

Tamara's voice broke through Lexi's thoughts as she led the spiral's small group of children into the main viewing area. "Decomposition of a whale fall occurs in three distinct stages, each of which benefits different marine species. The first stage allows animals like hagfish and sleeper sharks to pull soft tissue (including the abundant fat stores) from the whale's carcass; this stage can last a few months or as long as 18 months. The second stage involves animals inhabiting the whale's bones; this stage lasts several months or possibly up to five years. In the third and final stage, bacteria decompose fatty composites within the bones, releasing hydrogen sulfide that feeds deep sea shellfish like mussels, clams, and snails. This final stage of whale decomposition occurs when only minerals are left from the bones, which provide a solid surface for suspension and filter feeders to settle on. This can last for a few decades or until there is no more available space on the bones because they are covered in these animals."

She locked eyes for a moment with Lexi, sharing an unspoken grief, then turned away, focusing on the children. Lexi slipped through a hatch, silence descending once again as she moved down the hall, far away from the curious children peppering Tamara with a dozen questions, fighting to find the best space to view the rapidly disappearing carcass outside.

No matter what was happening in the world above, Casa Oceano's original purpose, that of the scientific study of the ocean and creatures within it, continued on. Above, the asteroid-induced nuclear winter continued to ravage Earth, sealing it in cold and darkness. Below, life continued on.

Lexi closed her eyes, her heartbroken still over the loss of Olanti. He was one of the best men she had ever known or had the honor to work with. She missed him more than words could express.

The overhead speakers chimed and Thetis announced, "Mayor Santfeli, your presence is requested in the Medical Bay."

A spark of hope chased the sadness away. Blanca had gone into labor early this morning. A rare miracle indeed as the ESH-positive survivors battled infertility. She was the first to carry a child this long and was heavy with Olanti's baby. Lexi headed for the Medical Bay, on the twelfth level of the spiral. She was so used to the multiple trips up and down the spiral each day that she was barely out of breath when she arrived, spurred those last few feet by the not-so-dulcet tones of a newborn.

She knocked, then entered the room. Blanca was smiling, despite her exhaustion. Swaddled tightly and tucked against her, a tiny babe lay close to her side.

"A boy." Blanca whispered, her eyes welling with tears of joy. "I wish Olanti could see him."

Lexi reached out a hand, stroked the tiny boy's cheek with one finger. She remembered sand and cliffs and a boy. Her friend. Her best friend. Hot summer days, barefoot, toes digging in sand and saltwater. She remembered laughter, adventure, and shared dreams.

"He can. Olanti sees him. He sees you, Blanca, he does."

Blanca gave a half sob, half laugh. "He was so excited when we learned I was pregnant. We had tried for over two years. Lost three. He still had hope. Told me he had a good feeling about this one. He said I had to believe it would happen. And he was right, it did." A tear ran down the side of her nose and splashed on the baby's face. The infant scrunched up his mouth, but his eyes remained closed.

"What's his name?" Lexi asked.

Blanca smiled down at the baby. His eyes opened then, and he stared up at his mother, a look of puzzlement on his face.

"Olanti Alexander Dimond." She met Lexi's eyes. "He once told me you were best friends and that he felt he was the luckiest man in the world, here at the end of our world, to live and work with his best friend, to have a chance at fatherhood and love. He would say, 'Azrael made it the end of one world, but

I think we must make it the beginning of another. How lucky am I to be given that chance?'" Blanca smoothed the blanket that swaddled her son. "I named our son not just after Olanti, but you as well, Lexi. For the friendship and love you shared. Olanti would want that. And I ask if you and Tamara will be his godparents?"

Lexi's heart broke all over again. *Olanti should be here. He should be with his son.* She gulped down the pain at the thought that her friend would never know the child he had made.

"It would be our honor."

Olanti Alexander Dimond was the first child born in Casa Oceano, but he wasn't the last. In the four years that followed, there were three more. The last child born, thanks to a donor who remained anonymous, was Tamara's and Lexi's. Lexi held four-month-old Aila in her arms as Demall Ataguri, her right-hand man since Olanti's loss, returned from the mainland, the submarine gently bumping on the platform.

"There are survivors. A small coastal town not too far from us."

Survivors. The impossible made possible. They weren't alone. Here on the spiral, it was easy to imagine they were the only ones left in the world. But Demall had discovered others. And there would be more. Lexi felt sure of that. Aila squirmed in her arms, her mouth pursing in a moue of discontent. Any moment now, she would demand to be fed.

Lexi tilted her head toward the entrance ramp and walked, Demall by her side.

"They have hundreds there. It's been so long since I've seen that many people in one place. And they say that there is a new nanite therapy that will reverse the sterility and fetal deaths."

"A new world awaits us, Demall. Washed clean, we begin again." Lexi said, and Aila whined in discontent, her whine building to a wail. She wanted food *now*.

"I only hope we can do better with this one than the last one." Demall replied.

"We will." Lexi replied, hope blooming in her heart.

Author's Note

As I began to write in this book, I found myself returning again and again to Maslow's Hierarchy of Needs. Simply explained, you can think of it as a pyramid. On the bottom level, is the physiological level, that of food, water, warmth and rest. The next level up, is safety and security. These are the basic levels of the pyramid, something that at the end of one world, and the beginning of another, becomes all-consuming. It spurred me to create a completely different hierarchy of needs - that of the writer. Something that is very prevalent on my mind as I write this Introduction now, in the first days of 2023. We all have a hierarchy of needs. To survive, to feel secure, to be loved (or read), to push ourselves farther, higher, always seeking, always reaching.

The hierarchy of needs I created goes from the ground up as follows:

Bottom level: To write and publish/share that writing

Second level: To be read

Third level: To be read by people I don't know

Fourth level: To break even (not spend more than I make publishing)

Fifth level: To make a profit (not huge, just not a loss)

Sixth level: Bestseller (hey, it would be nice)

Seventh level Apex: Make a living writing

As I continue my progress in moving through my hierarchy of needs, I hope you will continue to join me on this journey. I'm currently working on the 4th level this year. Fingers crossed; I might actually move into the 5th level!

There is one further book in this series. I hope to see *G581: Zarmina's World* published at the end of the year.

Please take a moment and review this book. Book reviews are social proof. They tell a potential reader that someone else has read it, and appreciated it enough to take time to write a review. It helps encourage them to take a chance on an unknown author.

And while you are waiting for *G581: Zarmina's World*, may I suggest you peruse my other books? The *War's End* series is interconnected and set in the earlier part of the 21st century. In fact, the Collapse is coming. It's just around the corner...*The Storm* is the first book in that series.

I love to hear from my readers. Drop me an email at shuckchristine@gmail.com or visit my author website at: https://www.christineshuck.com/ to join my monthly newsletter and receive exclusive access to short stories and more.

Thanks again for reading *G581: Plague Tales*!

Christine

Don't miss out!

Visit the website below and you can sign up to receive emails whenever Christine D. Shuck publishes a new book. There's no charge and no obligation.

https://books2read.com/r/B-A-BOLF-YZQFC

BOOKS 2 READ

Connecting independent readers to independent writers.

Also by Christine D. Shuck

Benton Security Services
Hired Gun
Smoke and Steel
Broken Code

Chronicles of Liv Rowan
Fate's Highway

Gliese 581g
G581: The Departure
G581: Mars
G581: Earth
G581 Plague Tales
G581: Zarmina's World

War's End
War's End: The Storm
War's End: A Brave New World
Tales of the Collapse
War's End Omnibus - Books 1-3

Standalone
The War on Drugs: An Old Wives Tale
Get Organized, Stay Organized
Winter's Child
Short-Term Rental Success

Watch for more at christineshuck.com.

About the Author

Fueled by homemade coffee ice cream, a lifelong love of words, and armed with strong female (and male) characters I cross genres like the Ghostbusters crossed the streams in pursuit of the question.

"What is the question?" you ask.

The question is simple. It asks, "What would you do, if..."

What would you do if you were fifteen years old and the world as you knew it fell apart? Would you run? Would you fight? Would you survive? – Meet Jess and her brother Chris in the *War's End* series.

What would you do if you had a chance to live your life over? Not just once, but twice? – Meet Dean Edmonds in *Fate's Highway*

What would you do if everyone you loved was lost to a terrible virus and you faced the real possibility of the extinction of the human race in the dark void of space? – Meet Daniel Medry in *G581: The Departure*

What would you do if hitmen were after you and you had no idea why? – Meet Lila and Shane in *Hired Gun*

If I don't keep you turning pages late into the night, desperate to know what happens next, then I have failed at my job. I'm a Taurus and born in Missouri. That makes me bull-headed and stubborn to boot. I don't believe in failure or mistakes, only learning opportunities and clever conversation. There's not much I won't do to make you burn the midnight oil reading my words while you suffer sleep-deprivation the following day. It's my secret superpower.

Born in flyover country, I've also lived in Arizona and northern California. I am an eclectic mix of snark and oddball humor. My colorful metaphors would make a fishwife blush. I'm an incompetent gardener, a dreamer and doer, in love with old houses and shooting pool, and chief organizer of all thing's household and financial. Feed me tiramisu and I'm yours forever.

Find me on all major platforms by visiting Linktree: https://linktr.ee/christinedshuck

Read more at christineshuck.com.

www.ingramcontent.com/pod-product-compliance
Lightning Source LLC
Chambersburg PA
CBHW071926190726
48293CB00004B/1184